"I'm sorry."

His voice sounded in her ear, and suddenly she realized how close he was. She could feel the heat of his body.

"I lost my temper. I shouldn't have said what I did."

As he spoke, the curls on her nape whispered softly against her skin, sending gooseflesh up and down her arms.

"You never told me about wanting a child."

It was true, she hadn't. But didn't every woman want children? He should have known.

His hand squeezed the flesh of her arm and heat kindled there. "I wasn't thinking straight that day on the stage. All those people watching. . . I just didn't know how to say it."

Her lips trembled, and she put a hand against them.

He turned her around and her heart caught. His broad chest was inches from her face, and she focused on one of the pearly buttons on his shirt. She couldn't bring herself to meet his gaze, though she felt it as sure as a touch. She closed her eyes, then felt his hand on her chin, tipping it up.

When she opened her eyes his gaze burned into hers, and her legs trembled under her. His eyes darkened to a deep bluish green. Their depths held a mix of sorrow and something else she was afraid to define. His thumb moved along her jaw, blazing a trail of fire. Her heart threatened to escape her chest. She closed her eyes again lest he see the depth of her feelings.

DENISE HUNTER lives in Indiana with her husband and three active, young sons. As the only female of the household, every day is a new adventure, but Denise holds on to the belief that her most important responsibility in this life is to raise her children in such a way that they will love and fear the Lord. The message Denise wants her writing to convey is that "God needs to be the center of our lives. If He isn't, everything else is out of kilter."

Books by Denise Hunter

HEARTSONG PRESENTS
HP328—Stranger's Bride
HP379—Never a Bride
HP475—Bittersweet Bride

Don't miss out on any of our super romances. Write to us at the following address for information on our newest releases and club information.

Heartsong Presents Readers' Service
PO Box 719
Uhrichsville, OH 44683

His Brother's Bride

Denise Hunter

Heartsong Presents

Dedicated to Colleen Coble and Kristin Billerbeck, my awesome critique partners and superb writers in their own right. You are my eagle eyes, my encouragement, my sounding board, my traveling buddies, and my dear friends. Love ya!

A note from the Author:
I love to hear from my readers! You may correspond with me by writing:

>**Denise Hunter**
>**Author Relations**
>**PO Box 719**
>**Uhrichsville, OH 44683**

ISBN 1-58660-845-2

HIS BROTHER'S BRIDE

All Scripture quotations are taken from the King James Version of the Bible.

All of the characters and events in this book are fictitious. Any resemblance to actual persons, living or dead, or to actual events is purely coincidental.

PRINTED IN THE U.S.A.

one

Emily Wagner untied the handkerchief from around her nose and mouth, breathing the undiluted dust for the first time of the day. The stage rocked over a rut, and she jostled the woman beside her. She thought to excuse herself, but after six days together and hundreds of such bumps, they were beyond the niceties.

Emily resituated herself as best she could in the fifteen inches space—less than that when she accounted for the heavy man on one side whose body overlapped onto her. She tried to wipe away the dirt she knew covered her face. When she'd dreamed of seeing Thomas for the first time, never had she envisioned her face streaked with dust and her hair a powdered gray.

She felt a trickle of sweat slip down her temple and wiped it away with the dirty handkerchief. To think she'd spent the last of her money on this ride.

It is money well spent, though, for it will bring me to Thomas. She smiled, her thoughts on her betrothed, then realized she was grinning stupidly at the scoundrel seated across from her. His knees, dovetailing with hers in the tight space, knocked softly against hers in a movement she suspected was not altogether necessary.

She wiped the smile from her face and looked down at her white fingers clutching her reticule. Thankfully, she was almost to Cedar Springs and her new life. She vowed she could not endure another day on this stage.

5

That was not entirely true, she reluctantly admitted to herself. In truth, she would endure anything to save her grandmother from her uncle Stewart's clutches. And this wasn't such a sacrifice at all.

She was eager to meet Thomas and have a real family at last. Thomas would be a wonderful father; she didn't have to see him in person to know that. They would have many children, and at last, she would have a real family, all her own. She cared not that the land Thomas farmed with his brother was not prosperous. She'd had little enough in Denver under Uncle Stewart's negligent care. She would make sure her new home was filled with laughter and warmth—and one day, the pitter-patter of tiny feet. *But first, though, I must find the gold. And soon, for Nana's sake.* She closed her eyes and tried not to think of what was at stake. She would not think of sad things today—when she was about to meet Thomas.

It couldn't be long now until they reached the town. She opened her reticule and withdrew the letter she'd saved for last. She'd reread one each day of her journey as a small reward to mark the time and lift her spirits.

She unfolded the paper, her insides churning at just the thought of Thomas's words. His bold, slanted script brought her familiar comfort. She held the page close to her, an effort to hide the private note from the woman seated beside her. Miss Donahue was quite beautiful but had a propensity to be somewhat nosy.

Focusing her thoughts on her intended, Emily read the words she'd nearly memorized.

> *Dear Emily,*
> *I am so pleased and honored that you have agreed*

*to join me in marriage. I know you will make a fine
wife and, Lord willing, a loving mother to any children
we bear. I hope I will not be a disappointment to you,
Emily, for you are deserving of the finest things in life.*

*Cade is happy for me, and we both look forward to
your arrival. It was generous of you to offer to look after
Adam during the daytime. It has been hard on my
brother, both losing his wife, and caring for a child and
a farm all at once.*

*Every day I thank God that your uncle found my
grandfather's letter. It is astounding that but for that one
missive, we would never have begun our correspondence.*

*I so look forward to meeting you in person. You have
been a great encouragement to me these two years.*

*I will expect you on in Cedar Springs, then, on the
eighteenth of May. I will be the man wearing a
proud smile.*

> *Fondly,*
> *Thomas*

Emily sighed happily and folded the letter. How many
women got to marry their dearest friend? She closed her eyes
and pressed the paper to her chest. *Thank You, Jesus. Thank
You for this man, for his willingness to marry me. Forgive me for
my role in this deceit. Help me to find success for Nana's sake.*

*Bless my union with Thomas, and Lord, bless us with chil-
dren. My heart fills to overflowing with thoughts of our babe in
my arms!*

The stage hit a rut and lurched. Emily grabbed the
hanging leather strap, her only means of support in the
center seat.

"Well, I'll be plumb tickled when this misery is over, I can tell you that," Miss Donahue said.

"Shan't be long now, if your destination is Cedar Springs, Kansas," said a gentleman behind her.

Emily's heart thudded heavily in her chest at the words. Her limbs felt weightless and jittery with anticipation. She turned, a difficult task with the heavy man at her side. "How long do you think?"

The man looked beyond her out the front of the stage. "We're coming up on the town even now, Miss. And 'tis glad I am to see it."

Emily turned quickly and looked just over the crest of a hill. A small town of mostly one-story structures loomed ahead. A few tall buildings and a church sat perched on a grassy hill at the far end of town.

Her mouth grew dry as her eyes scanned the approaching town. There were folks here and there, and numerous wagons, some parked, some moving. Where would the stage stop? Was Thomas waiting even now as he'd promised?

She glanced down at her watch pin. They were nearly forty-five minutes late, but that was to be expected. They entered town, passing over a bridge, the horses' hooves clopping loudly. The heat was forgotten. The dust was a dull memory as she looked ahead.

They approached a tall, white structure—Cooper's Restaurant and Boardinghouse, according to the sign—and the horses slowed to a walk. A few folk lingered on the porch, and her stomach fluttered at the sight of a tall, dark-haired man among the others.

It was him, it must be. He was the only man except for an elderly gentleman. His skin was darkened like a farmer's, though she would not have described him as gangly, as he had in one of his letters.

The stage drew to a sudden halt, and Emily was forced to take her eyes off Thomas long enough to steady herself with the hanging strap. Her torso pitched forward then back as the carriage settled in place. The woman next to her stood, eager to exit the stage, and Emily could see Thomas no longer.

She withdrew her hanky one last time and tried to wipe the dust from her face. When she brushed at her skirt, dust billowed from it. Oh, how she wished she were wearing clean clothes! And her face and hair must be a sight.

The driver opened the door, and the passengers began filing out, though most would be staying only long enough for the noon meal. Emily stood when there was room, then inched along the aisle, stooped over like an old woman because of the low ceiling.

Her stomach stirred with anxiety. What if Thomas thought her plain or homely? What if he changed his mind when he saw her? The thoughts tumbled through her mind and settled heavily upon her heart.

When she reached the stage door, the driver assisted her down, and Emily immediately sought Thomas's gaze. His own eyes, though, had settled on Miss Donahue, who was in front of her. The woman wore a hat over her dark hair, and Emily realized Thomas had mistaken the comely woman for her.

A cold, hard lump formed in her stomach. Of course he'd be hoping the beautiful Miss Donahue were his wife-to-be.

When the other woman rushed past Thomas and embraced the elderly man and woman, her betrothed's gaze left and scattered around the remaining travelers. His gaze settled upon hers when she stopped a few feet shy of him.

He was handsome; there was no getting around that. His dark hair reached just below his jawline on either side of his face, and his eyes, just below the rim of his hat, were a curious mix of blue and green.

A smile tilted her lips; she was unable to suppress her delight at meeting him at last. Everything in her wanted to embrace him. She knew him so well, and he her. She'd bared her heart to him on many occasions.

"Miss Wagner," he said loudly, speaking over the crowd of people. He removed his hat, and Emily noticed for the first time that he was not smiling. His lips were drawn instead in a tight line.

Her smile faltered. Why was he being so formal? Surely they had progressed beyond the formalities. "Emily," she corrected. They were to be married, after all.

He nodded once. "Emily. I hope your trip was uneventful. I'm afraid I. . ." He cleared his throat, his gaze breaking contact with hers. He twisted the brim of his hat between strong fingers.

His awkwardness was beyond endearing. She found herself smiling once again. Of course, he was simply nervous, just as she. Emily cupped his arm with her hand. "Oh, Thomas, I am so glad to be here." She tilted her head and affected an impish grin. "And not just because the ride was most dreadful."

"Emily, I have to tell you—"

"These your bags, Ma'am?" The driver set two satchels at her feet.

"Why, yes, thank you."

The stage crowd bustled into the restaurant leaving her alone with Thomas. The sudden quiet pressed in around them. Something was wrong; she could see it in his eyes.

Perhaps he was disappointed; she was no Miss Donahue, after all. The thought stung, but she could imagine what the heat and dust had done to her average appearance.

"I must look a mess." She tucked a stray hair behind her ear.

"You're fine, it's not. . . I'm afraid I. . ."

He stopped abruptly and, for the first time, a fire of dread burned within her. His hollow eyes spoke of more than uneasiness or disappointment. Liquid heat surged through her limbs and up her spine. "What is it, Thomas?"

His eyes were shrouded with emotion. She tried to read them, tried desperately to determine what had him so upset.

"I'm not Thomas." He cleared the raspiness from his throat.

"Not Thomas?" Was that all? Did Thomas have to stay behind at the farm? Perhaps he was afraid she'd be offended. Suddenly she realized who he must be. "Cade?" A hesitant smile formed. Relief began flowing through her, cooling the raging fire of dread.

"Yes, Ma'am, Cade Manning." He held out his hand, and she clasped it with her own.

His hand felt big and strong, his grasp firm, yet gentle. "Was Thomas unable to get away? I understand completely, please don't think I'm upset." Her reassuring smile was not returned.

"Miss Wagner—Emily." He met her gaze directly, and she realized he had not let go of her hand. "Two days ago Thomas's wagon tipped over into a deep ravine. He was thrown off. Apparently his head struck a stone or tree. . . ."

Emily's thoughts slurred. She tried to focus on what he was saying, but panic reverberated in her mind. *Wagon tipped. . .struck a stone. . . No. No, it can't be.* She shook her head and forced herself to speak. "What are you saying?"

His eyes were laced with sadness and something else. Pity, she realized through a fog of fear.

"I'm sorry, Emily, but there will be no wedding." His Adam's apple bobbed once, and shadows danced in the hollows of his cheeks as he clenched his jaw. "Thomas is dead."

two

Dead? Emily's mind faltered on the word. She felt her knees begin to give way. Her thoughts swam.

Cade caught her arm with a strong grip. "Whoa, there."

She felt his hand at her back, was aware of him guiding her away from the street. He was speaking, but his words came as if from some deep cavern.

Not Thomas, Lord! Not her dear friend in whom she'd confided. The only godly man in her life. What would she do now without him? She'd spent all her money to get here, and now there was no Thomas to meet her. No friend to marry.

Her thoughts careened wildly before coming to an abrupt halt. If Thomas were dead, she wouldn't be able to search his house for the map.

She didn't even have a way back to Uncle Stewart and Nana. She would have to tell her uncle she'd failed. That his plans were ruined. And what would he do then?

Poor Nana. How could Emily let Uncle Stewart put her in the asylum? But what choice would she have when she'd failed to find the gold?

"I'm sorry," Cade said. "I shouldn't have told you so sudden-like."

Emily looked at him. She was sitting on a bench beside him and wondered idly how she'd gotten there. Her satchels sat at her feet.

Her eyes stung as she looked into eyes that were probably

13

very like Thomas's had been. This man had lost his brother not two days hence, and the pain was still written plainly on his face. She remembered his wife had died in childbirth a few years back, leaving him and his little boy alone.

Guilt swarmed her mind. How could she be so selfish as to think of her own predicament?

"I'm sorry for your loss," she said. "You must be missing him mightily."

He propped his elbows on his knees, and his gaze found the planked porch. "He was a good man. A faithful man." His fingers played with the worn brim of his hat. "He cared a great deal for you."

Emily felt her face grow warm at his perusal. She'd cared for Thomas too. She had never known a person could care so much for one they'd yet to meet.

"He was champing at the bit about your arrival. Couldn't talk of much else for days."

Emily let the silence fall around them. She thought of the letters in her reticule and pulled the satchel closer to her body. It was all she had left of her friend. She felt like part of her had died. And in a way, it had. For Thomas had been dear to her, and she'd dreamed of a new life with him. Dreamed of children of her own. And now that dream was dead.

She looked around the town, trying to clear her mind. She had to think practically. She was on her own in a foreign town with no money and no family. *I have to get back to Nana and somehow explain to Uncle Stewart what has happened.*

"You must be hungry."

Her stomach recoiled at the thought of food. She shook her head.

"Well, you'll be wanting to head home, I reckon. I'd like to pay for the stage back to Denver and a room for tonight, if need be."

Her heart caught at his thoughtfulness. Did he know she was nearly penniless? But she knew Thomas and Cade barely made ends meet with their farm. "I couldn't let you do that."

"Thomas would have wanted me to."

She opened her mouth to argue but closed it. What choice had she? "Thank you kindly," she whispered.

He stood. "You stay right here, and I'll make arrangements."

She managed a smile of gratitude before he turned and walked into the establishment. Her heart felt smothered with sadness. She would never meet Thomas. He would never hold her or give her the children she so desperately wanted. Tears stung her eyes. She'd thought to have a new life, but she would be going back to her old one. Only this time it would be far worse, because she had failed her uncle.

Oh, Nana, I'm sorry. I tried my best, but I've already failed you, and now Uncle Stewart might send you away for good.

It wasn't fair. Her grandmother wasn't dangerous to herself or anyone else. She was only befuddled from time to time. There was no help for that. But she deserved to be loved and cared for, not locked up like a mad woman. Her uncle didn't care about her grandmother, though. He'd gained guardianship so he could acquire her home and possessions.

Emily watched a wagon clatter by on the dirt road. The white chapel, perched on the grassy knoll, seemed to watch over the town like an eagle watches over her young. Across the street, two men loaded sacks onto their wagon bed, their muscles straining against their shirts. She could picture Thomas here, in this quaint town of Cedar Springs. He'd described it to her in his letters, and his words came alive before her very eyes. His house and farm would have been no different. *You'll love the grassy meadows and rolling hills,* he'd written.

When Cade appeared again at her side, he took her hand and helped her from the bench. She noticed she scarcely reached his shoulders.

"It's all arranged. There's no need for you to stay here to-night. The stage leaves right after the noon meal for Wichita. From there, you can catch another stage back to Denver. If you'll follow me, I'll take you to Mrs. Cooper. She'll take care of you."

She followed him to a counter where a very attractive middle-aged woman stood. After introductions, the woman picked up Emily's satchels. "Cade said you might like to clean up. You can rest a bit until your stage leaves, if you like." She turned and made for the stairs. "Right this way, Miss."

Emily turned awkwardly to Cade. He replaced his hat and extended his hand. "Good luck to you, Emily."

His hand surrounded hers with warmth. She could feel calluses against the softness of her palm. "And to you." With that, she turned and retreated up the stairs.

After closing the door behind the kindly woman, Emily sank onto the soft bed and stared at the patterned wallpaper. Its swirls and whirls seemed to echo the directions of her thoughts. Even sitting here now, she couldn't believe it was true. Thomas was dead.

"Why, God?" she whispered to the empty room. He was so young, with a full life ahead of him. She'd been so looking forward to meeting him in person. They would've been so close, she just knew it. And she longed for a close relationship. She'd felt alone ever since her mama had passed on. Even Nana, dear though she was to Emily, had not filled the loneliness because her confusion and memory loss prevented a normal discussion.

She detected the aroma of fried chicken on the air, and her stomach turned. Though she'd not eaten since dawn, she knew she couldn't force down a single bite. She needed to gather her thoughts, to figure out what she was going to do.

She reached into her reticule and pulled out her diary. Whenever she needed to sort her thoughts, that was what she did.

Dear Diary,

I scarcely know how to write the words that I heard only minutes ago. I don't want to write them, for I fear putting them into print will make it more real. But that is what needs to happen. Perhaps then the truth will begin to sink in.

Thomas is dead. I learned the dreaded news upon my arrival in Cedar Springs. Thomas's brother, Cade, met me at the stage stop. He looks a bit as I thought Thomas would, though he's sturdier than Thomas described himself. I will never forget the look in Cade's eyes. I have never seen such emptiness. And as I remember the loss of his wife several years ago, I know that Thomas's death must have dealt a harsh blow to him.

I have only minutes to decide what I am to do. Though, I suppose, there is really little choice in the matter. Cade has graciously agreed to pay my fare back to Denver. It's a good thing too, because I am nearly penniless at the moment.

Only the thought of facing Uncle Stewart makes me question my decision. What will he do when he

discovers I have not been able to follow through with
his plan? Never mind that it is no one's fault. He will
somehow find a way to assign blame to me. I don't
fear for myself, but I do fear that he will take his
anger and disappointment out on Nana.

From below, she heard the sounds of chairs scraping across the floor and knew her stage would be leaving soon. She packed the diary back in her bag and took a few minutes to freshen her appearance before leaving the room.

❧

"Gee-up!" Cade snapped the reins, and the horses began walking, kicking up the dry Kansas dirt. He paid no heed to the direction he went; his bays knew their way home.

The familiar knot in his stomach coiled tighter the farther he got from town. He hated leaving the woman there alone. She'd walked away from him, following Mrs. Cooper up the stairs, her shoulders slumped, her head down.

Thomas had not told him much about Miss Wagner's life in Denver, but he wondered if she had much to return to back home.

When she'd gotten off the stage, he'd been taken with her obvious awkwardness. Her chin had tipped down, and he'd dreaded telling her about Thomas. She'd come all that way thinking her future was secure, and he'd had to tell her otherwise.

And when she'd mistaken him for Thomas, his own heart clenched. He shook his head. It had been one of the most difficult moments of his life. These past two days had been almost more than he could bear. Of course, he was acquainted with grief. When he'd lost Ingrid, he'd thought his body would wither up and die with the pain of it. But he'd had Adam to care for and raise. And the women in town helped out a great deal. Some of the townsfolk cared for baby Adam while Cade resumed farm work, but they had their own lives, their own families to care for. Eventually, Cade assumed full responsibility for Adam. And his brother was there to pick up the slack around the farm when he had to tend to his son.

But now Thomas was gone. It was only he and Adam. How would he manage the farm and his busy five year old? Even if he got neighbors' help for awhile, how would he manage every day, month after month, year after year? He tried to picture his daily routine without Thomas. He would prepare breakfast as usual. But Thomas had always milked the cow, collected the eggs, and slopped the pigs while he'd fixed breakfast. Now he'd somehow have to do all that. And the laundry, mending, cleaning, and butter-making. And, with spring arriving, the land had to be plowed and the seed planted. That alone was a dawn-to-dusk job, if he wanted to have enough harvested to keep them all winter. How could he manage Adam with all that? He and Thomas together had scarcely managed to get all the work done.

Lord, I can't do all that by myself, he prayed.

He rubbed his chin and felt the scruff from the past couple days. His mouth was dry, his throat tight. He sighed heavily, rocking on the seat as the wagon cleared the ruts in the road.

Sara McClain was at the house with Adam now, and he knew she would offer to help out. But he needed more than help. He needed a full-time worker. He needed someone to care for Adam while he worked in the fields. He needed someone to do some of the chores around the house. He needed. . .

A wife.

The word hit him square in the gut. He didn't want a wife. He felt as if he still had one. *Ingrid.* His heart still belonged to her. It seemed wrong to even think of taking another woman. It seemed like a betrayal.

She's gone. I know that, and losing her was too hard. Too painful. I don't want to go through that again. Loving hurts. Hadn't he loved Ingrid and lost her? Hadn't he loved Thomas and lost him too?

But he needed help, there was no denying that. There were practical matters to consider here. He didn't have the luxury of getting his life the way he wanted it; if he did, he would be on his way home to Ingrid even now.

One of his bays whinnied and scuttled around a deep groove in the road. The afternoon sun beat down on his skin, and a trickle of sweat rolled down his face from beneath his hat.

What was he to do? If he took a wife, it would have to be an arrangement of sorts. He couldn't give himself to her the way he had to Ingrid. But what woman would marry under those circumstances?

Emily.

His grip tightened on the reins. He thought of Thomas's words about his intended. He'd read parts of her letters aloud, so Cade knew a little something about her. And somehow, he knew, Thomas would have approved of Cade taking care of Emily. He'd once said there was some sort of strain between Emily and her guardian uncle.

He rubbed his chin. Could this be the answer? Would Emily agree to such a thing? His heart caught in his chest even as his thoughts bounced to and fro. It might work. She might agree to marry him, and then Adam would have a woman to nurture him the way only a ma could. He wanted that for his son.

He would do it. He would ask her. The worst thing she could do was say no. He noted the sun's position in the sky and drew in a quick breath. The stage was leaving after the noon meal. And Emily would be on it.

He pulled the reins to turn the horses. He had to get back to town and fast.

"Yaw!" he cried, and snapped the reins.

❧

Emily made her way out to the porch with her two satchels in hand. She felt clean after washing the dust off her skin and brushing the dirt from her hair. She'd wanted to change her dress, but the other two in her case were in no better condition. So she'd made do and beat the dirt from the material with her brush.

Her fellow travelers were entering the stage, so she handed her satchels up to the driver. She would wait until the very last minute to board herself. The thought of three more days on the stage was almost as daunting as the thought of returning home to her uncle.

"Board!" the driver called as he hoisted himself up onto his seat.

She reluctantly stepped up into the stage and took the only seat left, the uncoveted middle bench. She settled the folds of her skirt and tried to avoid the gaze of the man who sat across from her.

The stage jerked forward as the horses were spurred on. A clatter at the side of her stage caught her attention. She looked out the window and saw a wagon pulled alongside the stage.

"Stop the stage!"

The words came from Cade, who balanced on the edge of

his seat as if willing to cut the stage's horses off with his own.

The stage slowed to a stop. The curses from the driver were muffled by the roof over her head.

"Whatever's the trouble?" Miss Donahue asked.

A man behind her sighed. "We're already behind schedule."

But Emily's mind spun with confusion. What was Cade up to? What if he'd changed his mind about paying for the stage? She would be stranded here with nothing, with no one.

Her traveling companions watched as Cade leaped off his wagon bench and hurried to the stage door.

"Oh!" Miss Donahue said.

The door flung open. His gaze darted around the stage and settled on hers. She saw a twitch of surprise and realized the last time he'd seen her she'd been a filthy mess.

"Can I have a word with you in private, Miss Wagner?"

"Well, I—"

"Get off and let us be on our way," one man said.

"I'm not leaving until I have a word with her." His gaze didn't leave hers.

Emily, drawn by the intensity of his gaze, began to rise.

"Then say your peace and be done with it," said someone behind her.

"Yeah, Mister, you're holding us up."

Emily settled back in the seat and tried to read his face.

"Very well." He removed his hat and looked down at where his foot was perched on the door ledge.

His gaze found hers again. "Look, Miss Wagner, it's like this. You came here needing a husband, a home. My brother can't offer that for you anymore."

Emily's heart stomped a hoedown in her chest. Her stomach tightened.

"I need a wife. My son needs a ma."

Out the corner of her eye she saw Miss Donahue's fan begin fluttering.

"We don't have much to offer." He looked down again, and Emily's throat constricted. "But we have a home where you'd be welcomed."

Emily could scarcely believe it. It was an answer to her prayers. Cade was a godly man; she knew that from Thomas's letters. He would be a good husband to her. She opened her mouth.

"Before you say anything—" He stopped and took in their rapt audience.

Emily, too, glanced around her. Miss Donahue leaned forward, her fan twitching erratically. One impatient man rolled his eyes, and two of the men in the back stared unabashedly, their arms crossed impatiently. She looked back at Cade.

"This could solve both our problems. I need to explain a few things, though—"

"Enough already!" the impatient man said. He glared at Emily. "Answer the man and be done with it."

Her body felt weightless, and her mouth went dry. "I. . ." She looked at Cade. "I—yes, I accept your offer."

She heard Miss Donahue draw in a sharp breath.

A smile spread wide across Cade's face. "I'm honored, Miss Wagner." He held out a hand and assisted her off.

"Get your own bags," the driver snapped.

Cade hefted down her satchels and set them at her feet as the stage lurched away.

"Best of luck to you!" Miss Donahue called out the window.

Emily turned to Cade, her face growing warm under his gaze.

"I'd like to find Reverend Hill and get this settled tonight, if that's agreeable to you."

She nodded.

He walked her to his wagon and set her satchels in the wooden bed. As he helped her onto the bench and walked around to mount up beside her, Emily couldn't stop the glimmer of hope that spread like sweet honey in her veins.

three

Reverend Hill winked at Cade. "You may kiss your bride."

Emily felt her face flood with heat as her new husband leaned toward her. His lips touched her warm cheek, and she pushed away a niggle of disappointment. He might be her husband, but they had only met today, after all. Still, she was not so naïve that she didn't know the intimacy they would share tonight. The heat in her face flooded outward to her ears, and she hoped they didn't glow red.

"Congratulations, Dear," Mrs. Hill, who'd graciously served as their witness, said. "You're most welcome to come back to the house with us; I made two pies this morning."

"Thank you kindly, Mrs. Hill," Cade said. "But I need to get back to Adam."

After they bade farewell to the older couple, Cade helped Emily onto the wagon bench, and they made their way to the farm. On the way there, Cade told her about Adam. Emily already knew he was five, and she was looking forward to taking care of him. She laughed when he told her Adam's favorite activity was playing in the dirt with sticks. "He's right fond of his marbles too," he said.

He told her about their farm. They had a milking cow, chickens, pigs, and the two horses that pulled the wagon. He was a wheat farmer, and they had a garden to the side of the house where she would grow corn, tomatoes, onions, and anything else she wanted to plant.

Cade seemed relaxed and serious as he spoke. But excitement stirred within Emily. She was a married woman now. Tonight, she and Cade would begin their lives as husband and wife. Soon, she would carry a child of her own, and her heart yearned for it. Not that she wouldn't love Adam; she thought she would love him as her own. But everything in her longed to carry a baby within her womb, to deliver a son or daughter and nurse the babe at her breast. And she wanted lots of children. She wanted a house full of laughter and teasing like she'd had as a child.

Cade turned the horses onto another road. "This is it."

The long road was packed dirt with tall grass on both sides. In the distance, a two-story white clapboard house sat, flanked by a barn on one side and a grove of trees on the other.

As they pulled up to the house, a boy burst through the door, followed by a petite woman with lovely dark hair. Immediately, Emily cringed as she thought of her own haphazard appearance.

"Pa!" Adam hardly waited for the wagon to stop before he clambered up into Cade's lap for a hug. "Who's she?"

"Adam, where's your manners?"

Cade introduced her as Emily but didn't mention she was his new wife. Emily figured it was probably best to wait until they were at least in the house before telling the boy.

He introduced the other woman as Sara McClain, a neighbor, and the two women exchanged pleasantries. Emily knew the woman must have wondered who she was and why she'd come to Cade's home, but to her credit, she didn't pry.

After the horses were put up and Mrs. McClain left, Cade took her into the house. Immediately, she could tell it was a man's home. There were no fripperies or bric-a-brac lying around. The furniture looked sturdy, but the room seemed almost barren. It was, however, recently swept. Probably by Mrs. McClain, she guessed.

After she'd looked around, she noticed Cade was speaking to Adam. "So now she's going to live here with us."

Adam glanced at Emily, and she smiled tenderly. "I hope we can be friends, Adam."

"I already have lots of friends." A thoughtful frown puckered his brow. His eyes were an expressive blue, and she watched as they studied her seriously. "I don't have a ma, though."

Emily's heart caught at the innocent expression on the boy's face. She sensed Cade going still at Adam's side. Was he afraid Adam would forget his real mother? Emily didn't want to do anything to hurt Cade, but the boy clearly longed for a ma.

She squatted down to his level. "You don't have a ma, and know what? I don't have a little boy. Maybe we can kind of fill the gap for each other. Would that be all right?"

Her gaze darted up to Cade's. He seemed to approve.

"Do you know how to play marbles?" Adam asked.

"No, I surely don't. Perhaps you can teach me."

Adam nodded. "Okay. I can teach you what boys do, and you can show me what a ma does."

Emily held out her hand, her heart squeezing tightly. "It's a deal."

Later that night, as Emily and Cade tucked Adam into bed, she hugged the boy. The straw ticking crackled with the movement. "Good night, Adam. Sweet dreams."

"Night, Emily."

She left the room, leaving Cade to say good night, and made her way down the stairs to clean up the mess from supper. As she pumped water into the basin, her thoughts drifted to the man upstairs. *My husband,* she thought, a giddy feeling racing through her. Thomas's brother. It was strange, how it had all happened. While her heart ached with the loss of her dear friend, she was married to his brother.

She shook her head, willing away the sadness over her loss. She had a husband and child now to look after. *And a treasure map to find.*

She chased the thought away. She wouldn't think of it now. Tonight was for her and her new husband to become one. Heat simmered in her belly as she considered what lay ahead for her. Her mother had told her very little on the subject, but what she had shared with Emily left her anticipating the night ahead. If she could only settle her nerves. She wondered how long it would take her to conceive. She hoped it would be soon.

She scrubbed the crust of okra from the pan and rinsed it under a flow of cold water. She heard a floorboard creak above her head and knew Cade must be leaving Adam's room. Her belly tightened as she anticipated his appearance.

She began scrubbing another pan and tried to calm herself. By the time she'd finished the dishes and dumped the water, Cade had still not joined her. Wasn't he coming back down? Maybe he was waiting for her to join him. Warmth kindled in her stomach, and her breath caught in her throat. She leaned over the kitchen lamp and blew out the flame.

❧

Cade threw the last pair of trousers from the armoire into the bag at his feet and sat on the edge of his bed. All his personal belongings were ready to be moved into Adam's room. Emily's bags were still downstairs, and he needed to bring them up for her. He would let her have this room, and he would sleep in Adam's bed, as he'd just told him. His son had been tickled pink.

He would have to go back downstairs, but he needed a few minutes to gather himself. It felt awkward having a woman in the house again. And not just any woman, but his wife. Not in the true sense of the word, he reminded himself.

He looked at the bed where he and Ingrid had spent many cold nights huddled together beneath the covers. It had brought him some comfort over the past five years to sleep in this bed, as if he could recapture her here. But now, Emily would sleep here, and he would have to leave Ingrid behind. He knew it was time. Past time. Five years was too long to hold on to someone who was gone.

A tap sounded on the door. Emily probably needed her things brought up to her room. He stood, walked to the door, and turned the metal knob.

Emily stood on the threshold, a vision in white. A smile trembled on her lips. The simple nightgown she wore was modest, but his face grew warm, and his gaze dropped to the floor. There, ten bare toes peeked from beneath a white lace hem. His mouth felt suddenly dry.

❧

Emily forced her eyes to meet Cade's when he opened the door. Everything in her wanted to turn and flee. Her breath came so rapidly that her chest heaved beneath the gown.

His eyes widened, his jaw went slack, then he looked down. He was embarrassed, she sensed it instinctively, and it only served to embarrass her further. Should she have waited for him to come to her?

His body blocked the door and she wondered why he didn't

move to let her in. She should say something, anything. "Is Adam settled?"

He nodded, though his gaze avoided hers. "He's fine."

Silence filled the hallway again. "Supper's all cleaned up."

He nodded. "Good, good. Find everything all right?"

"Yes." Her skin was growing warmer by the minute beneath the gown. She felt flushed and wondered if he could tell. No, he would have to look at her to tell, and he was looking anywhere but at her. Wasn't he going to take the lead? Isn't that what husbands were supposed to do? She bit the inside of her cheek. She would just have to say it. "May I come in?"

He looked at her then. His eyes widened again ever so slightly, and his lips parted as if he were about to speak. Instead, he stepped aside. Far aside, giving her a wide berth.

She stepped through the door into the small room. One lantern by the bed cast a dim light in the room. Shadows danced across the quilted bedspread, across the wooden floors. The room was clean and sparse, even more so than the rest of the house, so her eyes went automatically to the bags that sat on the floor. Clothes spilled from one bag while the other was topped with a daguerreotype in a wooden frame. The woman in the picture stared somberly back at her.

His things were all bundled up together there on the floor. She cast another glance around the room. There wasn't a single item on the armoire or night table. Her gaze found the bags on the floor, then Cade's face. He'd packed up all his things. But why? A cold dread settled heavily in her stomach.

"I thought you might be more comfortable in here."

In here? Of course she'd be more comfortable in here; where else would she go? The barn? She searched his face, but his eyes were avoiding hers.

"I'm fixin' to move to Adam's room."

Confusion muddled her mind. He wasn't sleeping here? He was moving out? But why? Her thoughts tumbled back to the scene on the stagecoach—mere hours ago. *Before you say anything. . .I have some things to explain. . . .*

Is this what he'd wanted to explain on the stage? That he wanted a marriage in name only? He should have told her so right then and there!

She'd come to him wanting their marriage to start right. She'd come to him wanting to please him. She'd come here. . . .

She looked down at herself, clothed in a thin nightgown, and remembered the way he'd averted his gaze upon opening the door. Her skin grew warm until she thought she might glow. She'd all but thrown herself at him, and he didn't want her. She was mortified.

She bolted past him, wanting to escape the stifling room.

He grabbed her arm as she passed. "Emily." There was gentle coaxing in his voice.

"Let go." *Lord, please just let me melt in a puddle and sink through these floorboards.*

"I'm sorry, I thought you understood."

She looked away from him—couldn't bear to let him see her face. *What a brazen woman he must think me, coming to him dressed so.*

"I tried to explain on the stage," he rasped. "But the others. . ."

Her legs felt weak, and she wondered that they supported her at all. His grasp gentled on her arm, and the skin beneath it felt so feverishly hot.

"It's not you, it's—I just can't. I'm sorry."

Her eyes stung, and she knew tears would soon follow. She

would not let him see her cry. Hadn't she humiliated herself enough this night? She gave a nod and tore away from him, dashing through the door and down the stairs. She wanted to run outside and keep going until she had no breath left in her. She settled for the porch instead.

The door creaked behind her as she closed it softly. Her eyes still stung, though they were as dry as the prairie after a long, hot summer. She walked on wobbly legs to the porch swing and dropped into it. *Please, Lord, don't let him follow me out here.*

She'd never in her life been so humiliated. What had possessed her to go to him that way? They were strangers, she and Cade. No matter that they'd been joined in holy matrimony, they'd only met that very day. *Who am I to presume what he wants? Perhaps he finds me repulsive.*

Her heart caught at the thought. The hollow ache in her stomach filled with pain. She wasn't very comely, she knew that. Her uncle had reminded her often enough.

She remembered the daguerreotype she'd seen in Cade's room. The woman—his former wife—had been lovely. She'd had golden hair and petite features. And those haunting eyes.

What did Emily have? Drab brown hair and plain features. She must look as appealing to him as a garden weed. She crossed her arms, feeling exposed. The night air had grown chilly, but it felt good against her warm skin. She wanted to stay out here all night. She wanted to stay out here forever.

How would she ever face him again? She'd come to his room practically begging.

She closed her eyes. She didn't want to think about it anymore. It was beyond humiliating. She was his wife now—even if in name only—and she had a job. She still had to find the treasure map for Uncle Stewart. She still had to take care of Adam.

For the first time, it occurred to her that if there were no intimacy, there would be no child. She would never feel a baby kick her from within. She would never bring her own child into the world. She would never hold a suckling babe in her arms. Her throat constricted with the pain of it.

Oh no, Lord Jesus, what have I done? In marrying Cade, she'd given up her one true desire, and there was no treasure in the world worth that.

four

Dear Uncle Stewart,

I'm sorry it has taken so long to write. There have been some changes you need to be aware of. When I arrived in Cedar Springs, I found, to my sorrow, that Thomas had recently perished in an accident. Before you get riled up, I will tell you that I have married his brother, Cade. I am living in his grandfather's farmhouse, so I have been looking diligently for the map these past three weeks.

I have many other responsibilities as well. Cade has a five-year-old son I am looking out for.

Emily paused, her hand steadied over the paper, and watched Adam out the window playing with a pail beside a pile of dirt. She wanted to tell her uncle how sweet and precocious the boy was and how much his presence warmed her heart. But her uncle would not care about that. She continued.

In addition, there are animals to feed and care for, a garden to start, and all the household chores. I spend every spare moment looking for the map. Cade plows the fields from sunup to sundown, so I am able to do so without suspicion.

Emily cringed even as she wrote the words. Guilt had built up within her more each day. It felt wrong to search through

Cade's private things. *Well, isn't it wrong of him to deny me of my own children?* She would never realize her dream because of his decision. Was it so wrong of her to help Nana? Her gaze focused on the paper.

I have asked Cade some questions about his grandfather, but he doesn't seem to know anything about the robbery. He describes his great-grandfather Quincy as a "scoundrel" and says he disappeared one summer day and was never heard from again. This must have been the day he and my great-grandfather stole the coins. Cade doesn't seem to know Quincy and Great-grandpapa stole the gold or that they were hung for it the following week.

Emily rubbed her hands over her face. She hated thinking about the past and her involvement in this mess. She sighed and began writing again.

How is Nana? Does she still lie awake singing "Listen to the Mockingbird"? Please tell her hello and let her know I'm thinking of her.

She closed her eyes against the sting. Uncle Stewart would do no such thing; she could almost guarantee it. Was he making sure she was eating properly? Was he being kind to her? She knew better than to ask.

I promise to let you know as soon as I find the map. Until then, please take good care of Nana.

Sincerely,
Emily

She looked over the last line and knew she was pushing things. He didn't like to be told what to do. But she was keeping her end of the bargain, and it was only fair that he did as well. She folded the note, tucked it into an envelope, and addressed it. Now she had only to take it to the post office.

As she and Adam rode to town on the wagon, they sang songs together. She taught him "Camptown Races" and "Pop Goes the Weasel." He had his pa's dark hair and coloring, but his eyes were clear blue, and she wondered if they were like his ma's.

Once they arrived in town, she parked the wagon outside the mercantile and went to post her letter in the adjacent building. She left Adam on the porch with another boy while she entered the mercantile for a few things. It was not her first trip to the store, but she still felt like a stranger in town.

There were a few women in the store, two she recognized from church.

"Emily." One of those women set down the bolt of fabric she'd been eyeing and approached. "Good afternoon. I'm Mara, we met at church."

"Of course." Emily smiled, and wished she'd taken time to fix herself up. She must look a mess after gardening this morning.

"I'm glad to see you. I've been wanting to invite you over to tea one morning."

"That would be delightful."

They set a time for the next day, and Emily finished her shopping. It wasn't until Mara had extended the invitation that Emily had realized she was lonely for adult company. A friendship would be like a balm to her soul.

That next week, Emily finished up the supper dishes while Cade repaired a chair on the sitting room floor. She could hear him driving in nails and knew Adam was probably sitting beside him, taking in everything Cade did. She admired the relationship between Cade and Adam. The boy watched his pa so closely and imitated everything he did.

Emily dumped the dishwater behind the house and gathered up her sewing. Even as she dropped into the sitting room chair, her eyes felt heavy with weariness. Her busy days were catching up with her. Trying to run the house, look after Adam, and search for the map were taking their toll. She'd barely gotten started on the garden, and she knew she'd have to focus her efforts on that soon.

She threaded the needle and grabbed a shirt of Cade's from the little pile.

In front of her, Cade drove a nail into the arm of the chair.

"Can I try, Pa?"

Cade shook the arm to test its strength then turned the chair. "Here, hold the nail like this."

Emily peeked up from her stitching. Cade molded the boy's fingers around the nail's body then picked up the hammer. "Put your other hand here." Adam put his hand on the hammer, though Cade didn't let go. Together, they drove the nail into the wood.

"I did it!" Adam said.

Cade set down the hammer and squeezed his shoulder. "I reckon you did."

"Look, Emily, I did it," Adam said.

Emily smiled. "You're growing up. Before you know it, you'll be as big as your pa."

The proud smile on the boy's face was a picture that made Emily want to chuckle. Her gaze found Cade's, and they exchanged a smile. He looked away before she had time to enjoy the private moment. It was the most attention he'd given her since that fateful first night of their marriage.

She poked the needle through the fabric and pulled it out the other side. It was strange, their relationship. Cade cared for Adam and gave him affection, and the boy clearly adored his pa. And Emily had grown to care for Adam even in the short time she'd known him. Adam was starting to return her hugs and search her out when he did something he was proud of.

But Cade and Emily—their relationship was hardly a relationship at all. It was more as if they were acquaintances who shared a house. They said "good morning" and "pass the potatoes" and "good night" and little else. And yet, they were husband and wife.

Each night as she lay in bed waiting for sleep to come, she thought of Thomas and how different her life would be if he were still alive. They'd have shared their lives in a way that she and Cade hadn't. He would've shared her bed and given her a passel of children.

Stop it, Emily, it does no good to think of what cannot be changed.

"Why you making a chair, Pa? We have enough already."

Adam leaned over Cade's shoulder, almost smothering him with his closeness. Most men, she suspected, would have nudged him back. Cade just kept working as if it didn't bother him.

"It's for Mr. and Mrs. Stedman. They need another chair, and I remembered we had one in the attic just needed a little fixin'."

The attic. Why didn't I think of that? Emily had searched all over the house for the map, and she'd come up with nothing. But the attic would be the perfect place to look. Didn't folks keep things from past generations in attics? There were probably trunks of old things up there, and surely she'd find the map among the relics.

"—over there, did you?"

Emily felt Cade's gaze on her and raised hers to meet it. She'd not been paying a lick of attention. "I'm sorry, what did you say?"

"Adam said you went over to the Stedmans' the other day."

"Yes, Mara had us over for tea."

He nodded and talked around the nail in his mouth. "Glad you're making yourself some friends."

Emily was glad too. She and Mara had struck up an easy friendship, and the afternoon had sailed by before she'd known it. Afterward, she'd felt guilty that she'd been making small talk with a neighbor instead of doing her work or looking for the map. But she'd needed someone to talk to; she hadn't realized the depths of her loneliness until she'd started talking to Mara.

Cade set the chair upright and gave it a shake. "That should do it." He grabbed Adam and tickled him, then swung him up in his arms. Adam's belly laughs filled the room. "All right, Mister, it's time for bed."

"Aww."

Another round of tickling quickly put an end to the complaint.

five

Emily tossed aside an old quilt, and a cloud of dust rolled up around her like a prairie storm. She coughed as the dust settled on her damp skin, clinging to her and making her itch. She'd already searched through three trunks in this stuffy old attic, and there was so much more to go through. So far, her search had turned up no map, but the historian in her wanted to go slowly through each batch of letters and box of collectibles.

There was no time for that, though. Already, she was putting off much-needed garden work. The laundry, too, awaited her, and the downstairs was in dire need of a good sweeping.

She constantly worried that Cade would notice her neglect of other chores. So far, he hadn't said a word, but she knew by looking at her neighbors' gardens that she was behind.

"I'm thirsty, Emily." Adam looked up from his spot on the floor. His eyes peeked out from under an old beehive bonnet that was perched on his head. An old Prince Albert overcoat swallowed his body. She nearly laughed.

"I see you've found some new clothes."

"These ain't new, Emily, they's got too much dust on 'em for that."

"These *aren't* new," she corrected.

"I know, that's what I said. Can I have a drink now?"

Emily drew in a deep breath, then coughed at the dust she sucked in. She could use a break herself, but she wanted to finish this one trunk before she started supper.

40

"Tell you what. Do you think you could get your own glass of water if I let you go down to the kitchen by yourself?"

Adam stood up and the bonnet fell off. "Yes Ma'am!"

"All right then, let's get you out of here." She helped him over all the piles of relics, then went back to work.

She felt like she was getting to know Cade's ancestors just by going through their things. The clothes were mostly homespun. Trousers and linsey-woolsey for the males and calico for the females.

She'd come across old bank papers and coins, simple jewelry, and an old Bible. She'd found a lamp that was perfectly good and decided she'd take it downstairs. Cade had complained the sitting room was too dark.

By the time she finished going through the trunk, she sat back on her heels and sighed. Would she never find it? The faded remnant of the map Uncle Stewart found in his father's things said the more detailed map was hidden in this house. It was the only way he'd known there was hope for finding the gold. And her uncle's map indicated the gold was buried on the Manning property. But it would be impossible to find it among the miles of hills and caves that encompassed the property. Why, the gold could be buried anywhere.

She looked around the dark room. The lantern she'd hung from a nail shed dim, yellow light on the stuffy space. There were a few little tables to look through and still a couple trunks she'd yet to open, but those would have to wait until tomorrow. It was getting late, and she needed to get supper on.

She began putting things back into the empty trunk, taking care not to rip the fragile fabrics. She'd just stuffed the last gown on top when a sound at the door reminded her she'd forgotten about Adam.

"Did you get your drink of water without spilling?" she asked, tucking the clothing into the trunk.

"What are you doing?" The voice was no young boy's.

Her gaze swung to the doorway. Cade's large frame filled it, his face washed in a glow of lantern light. A frown puckered his brows.

Emily's mouth felt as dry as the dirt that coated her gown. "Cade, I—why, you're back early, I don't even have supper on yet."

He looked around the room as if to make sure everything was still there. She felt her face flush.

"Adam said you were up here."

"Yes, I—I wanted to sort through things." Her mind fished for a plausible excuse. Why hadn't she thought of this before? "I found a lamp for the sitting room." She held it up by the metal handle, but she felt the smile on her lips wobble.

He nodded, but the frown remained. She knew she must look a sight, evidence she'd been up here far too long to justify the finding of a single lamp.

"Well, I'd best get supper on." She began to rise, but her feet had fallen asleep and refused to support her. She reached out to grab hold of something, but there was nothing but air. She tried to take a step toward the wall, but her foot connected with something, and she tripped.

Cade stepped forward and caught her as she fell into his arms. Her hands found the hard flesh of his arms. His chest was a rock-hard wall against the softness of her cheek. Her pulse skittered.

He felt warm against her already heated body. She pulled back and realized his hands encompassed her waist. The glow of the lantern light flickered over his face, revealing something new in his expression. Her mind was too befuddled to put a word to it.

Her thoughts swirled in her mind in a heated frenzy. She felt his hands tighten on her waist, and it brought the oddest of sensations to the pit of her stomach. Her heart, too, reacted to Cade's nearness.

As his gaze roamed over her face, she became aware of how she must look. Dust and cobwebs probably coated her hair. She wondered if there were streaks on her face where drops of sweat made trails through the dirt.

She looked down, and her gaze locked on a button on his shirt. She felt his hands leave her waist, felt him pull back, both physically and emotionally.

Whatever she had seen on his face before was certainly gone now.

Her gaze darted to his, and she saw her suspicions confirmed. A deep shadow had settled into the plane of his jaw and shifted as his muscles twitched. His eyes too had grown distant, hard.

The silence swelled around them, and she wished he would say something, anything. Because she couldn't seem to form a rational thought.

She backed away a step, and her foot connected with something on the floor. She caught herself quickly.

"Pa," Adam called from somewhere downstairs.

Cade glanced at the door, then back to Emily. "Be right there," he called to Adam. His voice sounded loud in the confinement of the attic. He cleared his throat. His posture was stiff, his gaze harsh. She wondered what had caused him to go from warm and pliable moments before to rigid and withdrawn.

"I told him I'd take him for a ride while you get supper on." His voice was clipped.

Emily nodded, her tongue stuck to the roof of her mouth.

He started for the door, and Emily felt a physical relief that he was leaving. Before the breath she'd inhaled found release, he turned.

In the shadows, his expression was unreadable. "In the future, you might spend more time tending the garden than sorting through junk."

The words hit their mark. Her face went hot and her skin prickled. She heard his heavy boots thudding down the stairs and thought her heart must surely be as loud. Shame uncoiled in the pit of her stomach and snaked through every part of her. He *had* wondered why she was up here sorting through his things. She looked down at the floor where the silly lamp sat. Her excuse for being up here seemed absurd. The garden lay outside barely touched, and she was in here going through old relics.

He must think her lazy or incompetent or daft. Why else would she let chores go undone while she snooped about in an attic? And all for nothing, too, since she'd come up empty-handed.

She heard the front door slam and was relieved he was out of the house. A quick glance of the room reminded her there were still trunks to go through. And like it or not, she would have to go through them.

But first, she had to get cleaned up and get supper fixed. And if it killed her, she would get it done before Cade returned.

❧

Cade balanced Adam in front of him and kicked Sutter into

motion. His heart still thudded heavily in his chest even while guilt flooded his soul. He relived the moment in the attic, then shook his head as if to dislodge the thoughts. Never in his wildest dreams would he have thought he was capable of those feelings again. It was wrong.

But it had felt so right for just those few moments. Right and good.

Stop it, Manning. He clenched his teeth and kicked Sutter into a gallop. Adam laughed as the wind hit their faces.

But it *had* felt right and good. When Emily's eyes had widened in the glow of the lamplight, his gut clamped down hard. Her dirt-streaked face had looked adorable, had reminded him of the first time he'd seen her, getting off the stage.

Then Ingrid's face had come into his thoughts. Her golden hair and sad blue eyes. Sad because he'd been thinking of Emily in the way a man thinks of a woman.

She's my wife.

In name only, his spirit rebutted. What would Ingrid think of him now? She'd loved him and given birth to their precious son. What right did Cade have to carry on with another woman when his wife had lost her life bearing him a son?

"Faster, Pa, faster!" Adam's voice mingled with the wind.

"This is fast enough." Cade held his son close to him and allowed himself to enjoy the softness of his little body. Before he knew it, Adam would be too big to ride tandem with him. One day, he would leave home and go off on his own. The thought tugged at his heart. And then where would Cade be?

Emily will still be with you.

Yes, she would still be here, Lord willing, but they would be like brother and sister sharing a house. His heart denied the idea. When they were in the attic awhile ago, she hadn't felt like any sister he'd known. No, your skin didn't flush and prickle when you held a sister in your arms.

He shifted in the saddle, feeling suddenly discomfited. She didn't feel like a sister at all, but more like a—

Wife.

His mind rejected the thought. No matter that his heart had felt alive for the first time since Ingrid had died— he would not let himself fall for Emily. Hadn't he loved Ingrid well, and what had that gotten him? A broken heart. He'd grieved for months like he hadn't thought possible. He'd never imagined such pain as he felt when he'd lain his head on her pillow and smelled her lilac soap. Or held his baby in his arms, knowing Ingrid would never have that chance.

He didn't want to feel that way again. Ever. No amount of pleasure was worth that, and if necessary, he would put up walls twenty feet high around his heart to keep her out.

six

Emily,

I'll not waste time with pleasantries as you did in your letter. It seems you have settled in that cozy little farm-house with a husband and his brat and forgotten why you're there to start with. You are not there to be a wife or ma. You are there to find the map and gold. That is the only reason you are there.

Since you have become so lax in your thinking, I am going to save you from your laziness by setting a dead-line. You have until winter's first frost to find the gold. Anyone with any wits about them could manage that. Unless you want your grandmother to be sent away, you'd best get to work.

Uncle Stewart

Emily's belly clenched, and her fingers trembled on the page. She sat down on the settee, glad she'd sent Adam out to play. She was beginning to despair of ever finding the map. She'd finished looking in the attic and around the house. It was only spring, but winter would be here before she knew it. What if she couldn't find the gold by winter? What if the map was not even here? Someone could have found it and thrown it out long ago for all she knew.

She heard Adam squealing outside and peeked out the window. He sat in the dirt watching some bug crawl along the ground. He coaxed it onto a stick and squealed again. Emily smiled. She longed to go outside and play with him, but now she felt compelled to search for the map.

She looked around the room for some area, some piece of furniture she hadn't searched already. She'd looked everywhere.

Maybe she was going about it all wrong. Maybe Cade knew something that would give her a clue as to the gold's whereabouts. Maybe he even knew of the map but didn't know its significance.

That's it. I'll see if I can find out something from him. It sure beat looking for a needle in a haystack. Especially when she didn't even know if the needle existed.

❧

Emily put another spoonful of potatoes on Adam's plate and smiled at him.

"Thank you," he said.

Her eyes met Cade's, and she read the approval in them. She'd been working with Adam on his manners. He was a fast student, ready to learn and eager to please. Keeping him clean, though, was a task she'd given up on. She'd learned to let him get as dirty as he pleased, then have him get washed up for supper.

She glanced at Cade, who was serving himself another slab of ham. He could put away food, that man, but still stayed slim and solid. Well, it was no wonder with the hard work he did all day. Her gaze fell to his hands, so strong and tanned. His fingers, squared at the tips, were long and so. . .masculine.

And still.

Her gaze found his, and she saw he was studying her. She'd been staring at his hands, she realized, and knew he must think her odd. She picked up her fork and worked a piece of ham onto it, feeling the burning in her face. He'd never said a thing about their embrace in the attic awhile back. But she'd thought about it more than she cared to admit. If Cade had thought much of it, she couldn't tell, for he'd been as distant from her as he ever had.

Her uncle's words flashed in her mind. *You are there to find the map and gold. That is the only reason you are there.* The weeks were slipping away, and she had to start questioning Cade, like it or not.

She glanced in his direction and realized Adam was telling him about a game she had played with him today. How could she steer the conversation toward the map in a way that wouldn't draw Cade's suspicion? Then an idea occurred to her.

"Perhaps tomorrow we could play a different game," she said to Adam.

His dark eyebrows popped up high. "What game?"

"Well, seeing as how you like dirt so much, perhaps I could bury some treasure. I could make you a map with pictures and see if you can find it."

"Real gold?"

Emily laughed and hoped it didn't sound as brittle as she thought. "Well, I don't have any real treasure, but maybe we could use buttons and just pretend it's real."

Emily glanced at Cade, hoping to jog some memory. If he'd seen a map lying around somewhere, maybe he'd think of it now.

"Can we do it now?" Adam asked.

"Finish your supper," Cade said. "Tomorrow's soon enough." He glanced at Emily then back to his son. "You might help Emily with the garden before you think of asking her to play."

Embarrassment washed over her. Now he thought she was

putting off her chores to play games with Adam. He must think her completely slothful.

She tried to regain her composure. "We'll do our work first, won't we, Adam?"

"Aww."

"None of that," Cade said. "If we don't grow a garden, what do you reckon we'll eat all winter?"

This was getting her nowhere. He'd not taken the hint about the map at all, and now they were on a different topic altogether.

"How about if I draw up the map tonight, Adam?" she asked. "Then as soon as we're finished with our chores, I can bury the treasure for you."

"Yippee!"

"Finish your peas," Cade said.

"Yes sir."

Later that night after Adam was in bed, Emily sat with a piece of paper, mapping out the backyard. Her trees looked more like inverted pitchforks, but she supposed Adam would be able to make it out.

She glanced at Cade where he sat reading his Bible. She needed to get him talking about his grandfather or the map. Surely he knew something that would be of help.

She marked the spot on the map where she would bury Adam's treasure and held it up in front of her. Would Adam be able to understand the pictures?

"What do you think of it?" She held up the picture for Cade. Across the room, his gaze lifted from the Bible to the picture she held up. He squinted, and she realized he couldn't see well from across the room. She got up and walked over to the settee where he sat.

Feeling brave, she sank down beside him and handed him the picture.

His lips twitched as he looked at it.

She felt amusement well up in her. So her picture did look like Adam had drawn it. Had she ever claimed to be an artist?

His lips twitched again.

"And what's so funny, Mr. Manning?" she asked, feeling suddenly playful.

He glanced at her then back to the map. "Why's there a porcupine in the middle of the yard?"

"That's a bush." She swatted his arm and wondered if she'd overstepped her bounds.

His laugh was disguised as a cough.

"And I suppose you could do better?"

He looked at her then, and the amusement on his face made her feel warm and cozy all over. "I'm not the one who offered to draw a treasure map."

His smile slid away slowly like the ocean's tide, but his gaze remained locked on hers. She felt her own fade away. The mantel clock ticked off time, and so did her eager heart.

He cleared his throat and looked back at the paper. "It's fine, really." He handed it back to her. "You've been real good to Adam."

She accepted the paper and suddenly realized how close they were sitting. Her calico gown draped over his knee, and she realized she liked the intimacy the image invoked.

"I've grown fond of him. He's a good boy."

Cade settled against the back of the sofa, and she was relieved he didn't seem to mind her closeness. "He is good. But I've been a little neglectful of the manners and such. He's learning a lot from you."

His approval brought a wave of pleasure to her belly. "He's a delight to me, I assure you." All this talk was wonderful, but she couldn't help but think of her uncle's last letter and his deadline. Perhaps now, while they were talking so nicely, was a good time to probe.

"Adam's been asking about his ancestors lately." It was true. He'd had a barrelful of questions about who owned the clothes and trinkets in the attic.

"That a fact?"

"Umm." She worked absently on the map. "I didn't know what to tell him."

He closed the Bible on his lap and laced his fingers behind his head. "Not much to tell, really. We're farmers, going back at least three generations."

He went on to tell her about his own parents. They'd been hard workers and plain folk who'd done well to raise a family and provide the necessities. When he mentioned his grand-parents, Emily's ears perked up.

"Don't know much about Grandpa Quincy 'cept he didn't much like to work. My pa said he was gone a lot and would turn up out of the blue. One day he just disappeared, and they never did know what happened to him. Eventually, they figured he was dead and put a grave marker on the hill out back."

She'd seen it weeks ago and had wondered about it. "Do you remember him at all?"

He shook his head. "I was young when he disappeared."

"You must have missed having a grandfather."

He shrugged. "It was odd. Nobody liked to talk about Grandpa Quincy much. When I'd ask my pa about him, he'd get all snippy. Grandma didn't cotton to talking about him either. I just figured her feelings had been hurt by his desertion. She had a hard life, trying to keep up the farm without his help."

"What do you suppose he did all those times he went away?" She glanced at his face.

His eyes squinted as if he could see into the past. "Don't know. I guess I figured he wandered around, liked his freedom."

He didn't know. She could see the honesty on his face.

Unlike me. A wave of shame washed over her. *I'm doing this for Nana, though. I have no choice.* She shifted in her seat and watched the material of her skirt slide off his leg.

"Have you ever looked through his things? In the attic, I mean?"

His gaze fixed on her, his brows hiked up beneath his dark bangs. "No. Grandma must've put some things up there, but I've never gone through the stuff." His eyes narrowed, and their depths were laced with suspicion.

She grew warm under his scrutiny and adjusted her skirts around her legs.

"Did you find something up there?"

"No." The word, too emphatic, popped out of her mouth before she could stop it. But at least that question she could answer honestly. "No, I just—I just wondered if you'd ever looked through his things and found some kind of explanation of what he'd done while he was away," she finished lamely.

"Don't reckon there's much to find. He was just a wanderer who didn't much want to be tied down to family and work."

She nodded, not wanting to agree verbally. It would be too much like a lie, and she'd had her fill of dishonesty. She decided to turn in for the night. As much as she'd enjoyed her talk with Cade tonight, it didn't take a genius to recognize the suspicion that lingered on his face. And she'd just as soon hit the hay before he started asking questions.

seven

"I found another one!" Adam called from behind the big oak in the backyard.

"Good job, Adam. There are only two more marbles." She wiped a dirt-coated hand across her sweaty forehead and caught Adam's look. "Silly me," she called. "I mean only two more nuggets of treasure."

She grabbed a weed and gave it a mighty yank, feeling satisfied when the whole thing came up, roots and all. The spring sun beat down on her dark hair with such intensity, she wished she hadn't left her bonnet on the front porch.

Adam dug through the dirt a stone's throw away. Though she'd wanted to hide buttons for treasure, Adam had wanted to use his marbles. She hoped they didn't lose any of them. He carried them everywhere he went; you could hear them jangling together in his pockets as he walked.

"My aggie!" Adam called.

Emily saw him hold his favorite marble up in the air, wearing a proud look on his face.

"You mean your treasure," she corrected, relieved that he'd found his favorite. "One more to go!"

He attacked the dirt with vigor, and she moved down the row of tomato plants, plucking another weed.

She'd reached the end of the row when Adam jumped up. "I found it, Emily!"

The marbles that had sat in his lap spilled to the ground.

He reached down to collect them and ran to her. "Will you hide 'em again?"

"Tell you what, if you fetch me my bonnet, I promise to hide your treasure again after supper."

"Yippee!"

"It's on the front porch."

He ran toward the house, his marbles cupped in his hands. Emily watched him go until he rounded the corner, then, turned back to her work.

She'd only uprooted two more weeds when she heard his cry.

"Emily!"

She jumped up from the dirt, her legs faltering from having been bent so long. She could hear him crying, and though it didn't sound like an emergency cry, it sounded serious.

She came around the front corner of the house to see him lying facedown on the wooden steps, still, except for the heaving of his torso. Had he twisted his ankle on the steps? Hit his head on the porch rail?

Please, Lord, let Adam be all right.

"What is it, Adam?" She squatted down beside him.

"My aggie!" He pointed at the gap between the rise and tread of the step.

A heavy dose of relief flowed through Emily. She put a hand to her booming heart.

"Oh, Adam, you scared the wits out of me."

"It fell out of my hand and rolled down there." Another wail escaped his lips, and he turned his tear-trailed face to hers.

"It's all right, Sweetheart, we'll get it." She sat on the step beside him and patted his shoulder.

He turned into her arms and melted into her embrace.

"It's all right," she said.

"It's my best one."

"I know, Honey, we'll get it." She pulled away and surveyed the crevice. There was no way a hand would fit through there. She grabbed the step ledge and tried to pry it up, but it didn't budge.

"Let's get Pa," he said.

She tried to loosen the board again and failed. "I'm sure I can do it. I just need to find the right tool. Stay here."

As she walked to the barn, she looked back and saw there had been no need to tell him to stay put. Adam was not going to leave his marble.

When she sat down beside him again, she had a heavy hammer in her hand. "Move back, now." She whacked under the ledge until it lifted. As she pried up the board, the rusty nails squeaked as they loosened their grip on the plank.

Sunlight poured into the cavity, bathing the stale space with light. Emily set the step tread on the porch.

"There it is!"

The green glass marble lay nestled in dirt below. She reached in through strings of cobwebs and grabbed it. As she pulled it out, something alongside the inner wall of the steps caught her eye.

She handed the aggie to Adam, and he threw his arms around her. "Thanks, Emily." With that, he ran into the house, the door slapping behind him.

Emily reached back into the crevice and grabbed for the canvas against the wall. Once she had it in her hands, she quickly withdrew it, dropping it beside her, and plucked off all the webs on her arm. She set the plank in place and hammered it back down.

Picking up the rumpled canvas, she stood and walked up the steps.

On the top step she froze. The canvas, browned with age, and blurred by water damage was a map.

She eagerly scanned the page. Yes. She could see where a crude house was drawn. At the top right-hand side of the page, an X was very clearly marked, though the drawings in the area around it were blurred. She flipped the map around. If this were the front of the house, then the X was behind the house to the west. But how far?

She studied the lines and indistinct images. There was simply no way of telling how far. But it looked like. . .yes, it looked like the lines around the X depicted a cave or a cliff wall. The gold might be buried in a cave on Cade's property. But there could be many caves! How would she ever find the right one? And once she did, how would she retrieve the gold?

She scrutinized the picture again, then hugged it to her chest. At least she had an inkling now of the direction it was in. And maybe there were only a few caves out that way. She could ask Cade a question or two and then start searching. Hope welled in her chest. Maybe she could find the gold and be done with this whole mess before winter. Uncle Stewart would release Nana to her care, and surely Cade wouldn't mind if Nana came here to live.

She so wanted to get this over with. She was tired of deceiving Cade. Perhaps he withheld his affections because he sensed her dishonesty. Perhaps when all this was finished, he would find it within himself to love her as a wife. Somehow, even though she cared greatly for Adam, she couldn't seem to let go of the desire to have her own children. Her heart harbored frustration because of Cade. What were a few white lies when he was denying her dream?

Finding the map put a hope in her heart the rest of the day. Later that night as Emily tucked Adam into bed, she ran her fingers through his soft, dark hair. He had a new freckle on his nose, a result of the hours spent in outdoor play. She wondered idly if a child of hers would have freckles. Probably so, since her own skin was fair and prone to them.

"I forgot to get your bonnet," he said.

"I think we both forgot, Sweetheart."

"Does that mean you won't bury the treasure tomorrow?"

She chuckled and ruffled his hair. "I'll still bury it. But not until after chores."

A shuffle sounded behind her, and she turned to see Cade in the doorway.

She leaned down and planted a kiss on Adam's cheek. "Sweet dreams, Adam. Good night."

Suddenly, he pulled her into his little arms. "Night, Ma."

The word caused her breath to catch in her throat. Her eyes stung, and as she pulled back from the boy, the sweet smile on his face stole her heart.

She squeezed his arm and stood, turning to leave the room. But before she took a step, her gaze connected with Cade's. His stricken expression impaled her. She couldn't move for a moment, caught in the steely web of his gaze. His displeasure was evident in the tight bunching of his brows, the rigid set of his shoulders.

Quickly, she brushed past him and down the stairs. She grabbed her sewing basket and busied her fingers with a holey stocking. Why was Cade so distressed that Adam had called her "Ma"? Was it so awful that he had grown to love her, that she had grown to love him? A child needed a mother, and she was the only one this child would ever have. That was his reason for marrying her, after all.

She realized the hurt she'd read on Cade's face must be on Ingrid's behalf. Of course that must hurt. But it had been five years, and it was only right that Adam should have a ma.

She stuck the needle through the material and pulled it out the other side. The look on Cade's face bore into her with more force that she'd like to admit. His displeasure bothered her. Wasn't she good enough for his son? Did he see something in her he disliked so much that he wanted distance between her and Adam? Wasn't the distance between her and Cade bad enough?

She heard his feet on the stairs and stiffened as he entered the room and settled across from her, his Bible in his lap. She kept her gaze fixed on her work. Her heart jumped against her ribs.

Cade's presence in the room was thick and tangible. The very air had changed when he'd entered, and her spirit squirmed. Did he regret marrying her? Her gut clenched at the thought. Did he dislike the influence she had over his son? When had she come to care so much what he thought of her?

Her gaze darted to him, and in the brief instant, she knew why she cared so much. She was falling in love with him.

She glanced at him again, her fingers trembling with the discovery. Was it somehow written on her face, in her posture? She felt sure it was and wished she could evaporate right then and there. She poked the needle through the stocking, and it poked her finger.

She sucked in her breath.

He looked at her then.

She looked at her finger, where a dot of red bloomed, and blotted it with a handkerchief from her pocket.

"You all right?" he asked.

She nodded, holding the cloth to stanch the flow of blood.

Quiet settled over the room like a heavy fog. She wondered if he looked at her still, but hadn't the nerve to check.

Upstairs, Adam shifted in his bed, and the straw ticking crackled. The mantel clock ticked off time.

"I'm sorry about how I acted upstairs."

She looked at him then, her heart in her throat. His expression was soft in the glow of lamplight, and her breath came in shallow puffs. He was so strong and masculine, yet sometimes she caught a glimpse of this gentle side and wondered at it.

"It's good for him to call you 'Ma.' " There was a glimmer of sadness in his eyes.

A dark cloud of jealousy spread through her, but she pushed it away. It was only normal that Cade would be sad for his loss. For Adam's loss.

❧

Cade wondered if Emily could see the heavy thumping of his heart through his shirt. When she looked at him like that, with her doe-brown eyes all defenseless, he remembered that time in the attic when he'd held her in his arms. The familiar stab of guilt stopped the thought.

He had to think about Adam now, and his need of a mother. He'd wanted his son to have a mother; that was a big part of why he'd married Emily to start with. But hearing his son call her "Ma," seeing him embrace her, had sent an ache deep into the pit of his stomach. Ingrid was not here to be his mother, and though it hurt to see her replaced, Emily was a fine substitute. She would love him and nurture him the way a child needed.

Emily's face was mask of vulnerability. Did she think he was angry with her? *Admit it, Manning, you were angry with her. Angry that she's replaced Ingrid in Adam's eyes.*

"You've been good to Adam," he said, wanting to allay her fears. "I reckon he's taken to you like we both hoped he would."

She pulled the handkerchief off her finger and surveyed the pinprick, then twisted the white material in her hands. "I've grown fond of him."

She wetted her lips, and he wished for a moment that she'd said the words about him. Had she grown fond of him as well? The thought made his heart jump.

As if she could read his mind, her face turned pink, and she looked down at her hands. "He's a good boy; you've done well by him."

The words struck a note of pride in his father's heart. He'd done his best, but Emily had given Adam something he'd badly missed. Gratitude for her swelled up within him. He'd gotten a mother for his child and a woman to care for all their needs, and what had she gotten in return? A place to live? How could he repay her for her sacrifice? He felt a deep longing to do something for her.

"I appreciate everything you've done for him. For us." He nodded and hoped the words hadn't been spoken too brusquely. Words were not his specialty, especially flowery ones.

"It's a privilege to care for Adam." Her gaze avoided his, and he thought he'd embarrassed her with his gratitude.

He wished briefly that she'd included him in her words. Did she count it a privilege to care for him as well? He knew the thought went beyond their relationship, but he wanted it to be true regardless.

"You don't mind then?" Hope lit the velvet brown of her eyes.

His thoughts, scattered as a whirlwind, missed her meaning.

"If he calls me 'Ma,' I mean," she said.

He shook his head. "I think that'd be best."

She gave a short nod and picked up her sewing. Somehow, allowing her to be a real mother to his son made him wonder what it would be like if she became a real wife to him. His gut clenched. With a clamped jaw and a tenacious spirit, he tried to call up pictures of Ingrid. Pictures of their own wedding, of her standing over a hot griddle, of her reading by lantern light. Deep down, in the shadows of his mind, he admitted that these days, those pictures were fading from his memory. And he wondered what would take their place.

ᴓ

That night before Emily snuggled up under her quilts, she pulled her diary from its drawer and sat back against her pillows.

Dear Diary,

What an eventful day this has been! Quite by hap-penstance, I found the map under a step on the porch. It is, unfortunately, damaged by water and weather, but it gives me the general idea of the gold's hiding place which is more than I had before.

Awhile ago, while I tucked Adam into bed, he called me "Ma" for the first time. My heart wanted to weep with joy. He is the child I always longed for, and though I didn't carry him in my womb, he is every bit the child of my heart. It was distressing for Cade to hear his son call me "Ma," but now, I think, he has decided it's best.

I'm hope this will bring our little family closer

together. For right now, I don't feel like we're a family at all, but rather like three people sharing the same abode. I can't help but think Adam feels this too. Perhaps with time, Cade's heart will soften toward me, and we will be a real family at last.

eight

Dear Uncle Stewart,

I have good news for you. I found the map that Quincy Manning hid. It was beneath the porch for all these years. Although it has significant water damage, I was able to tell the general direction to search for the gold. It looks as if they buried it in a cave. I have inquired of Cade about the caves on his property as much as I can, but I don't want him to become suspicious. Because of the map's condition, I'm not sure how many caves there are to search, but most of them appear to have numerous tunnels.

Though the summer is well under way, I'm hopeful that I will meet your deadline. When I find the gold, I will notify you right away. Perhaps then Nana can come here, and you won't be burdened with her care any longer. Please take good care of her for me and give her my love.

Sincerely,
Emily

Emily stashed the letter in the envelope and sealed it. A dose of guilt trickled through her veins, and she knew Sunday's sermon was the cause of it. Had Reverend Hill's sermon on Potiphar's wife been just for her? It had been awhile since she'd heard the story of Joseph and how Potiphar's wife had tried to seduce him. Although Joseph had turned her away, she deceived her husband and told him Joseph had tried to seduce her. The sermon had focused on how God had blessed Joseph regardless of the evil done against him, but a different point poked Emily in the heart. She was deceiving her own husband just like Potiphar's wife had.

But this is different. I'm doing it for Nana's sake. Potiphar's wife was doing it for her own selfishness.

It wasn't as if Emily was after the gold herself. She wanted nothing to do with the stolen gold. She wanted only Nana's safety.

But I'm deceiving Cade.

She couldn't get around that no matter how hard she tried. Did the end justify the means? It was a question she wasn't sure how to answer. She felt like the raccoon she'd seen two dogs chase up a tree this week. What choice had she? Was she supposed to let her uncle put her grandmother in the asylum? Dear, gentle Nana? Her stomach twisted. *Help me, Lord.*

But even as the words formed in her mind, she snatched them back. There was no easy answer here, no way out of this dilemma. She would just find the gold as quickly as possible; then she could get on with her new life here. Life as Adam's mother and Cade's—she couldn't quite bring herself to say the word. She was not Cade's wife at all. But in the depths of her heart, she knew she longed to become his wife in every sense of the word.

ঽ

Emily took a sip of the tea Mara had poured her and watched Adam playing with Beth, Mara's little sister-in-law. Though Beth and Mara weren't related by blood, it was obvious they shared a mother-daughter bond.

Mara settled in the swing and dragged a hand across her forehead. For the first time, Emily noticed that her normally peachy skin was blanched.

"Are you feeling peaked?" Emily studied her friend, noticing a bead of sweat roll down her temple even though the summer day was mild. "You seem tired."

Mara sent her a private smile, then her gaze swung to Beth who was showing Adam how to balance his marbles on the fence post. "I'm fine really. In fact, I—" Her face reddened. "I am in the family way." Her smile widened, and her face softened with excitement.

A baby. Mara would be having a baby. Emily's heart caught with a mixture of joy and envy. "Oh, Mara, that's wonderful!" she exclaimed, feeling a prickle of guilt for the part of her that cringed.

Mara laid a delicate hand on her flat abdomen. "I just told him last week." She giggled. "He's so excited. Beth too."

Emily took a sip of her tea, wishing for the world she could swipe away the ugly envy she felt. She already had Adam, loved him; why couldn't that be enough?

"I just can't get over it sometimes. God has blessed us so much. I feel so undeserving."

Emily had heard others talk about the change Mara had experienced when she'd asked Christ to lead her life. She had trouble believing the woman beside her used to be as self-serving and uppity as they said.

"I hope the good Lord blesses us with a whole passel of children." She laughed. "I know, it's easy for me to say now. I have yet to experience even one."

"You'll be a wonderful mother. You already are. Look at Beth. She adores you."

"She's a joy, sure enough. I count her as my own." Her gaze bounced off Emily. "But—I don't know if I should even say this, it's probably wrong but. . ."

"What is it?" They hadn't known one another very long, but already, Emily felt close to Mara.

"Well, as much as I love Beth, I've longed for a baby of my own."

Emily felt her skin prickle with heat. She grabbed Mara's hand. "Oh, Mara, I'm so relieved to hear someone else voice the same feelings I have." Her eyes stung with the fervency of her feelings. "I love Adam, I do. But—"

"But there's something about carrying your own child, about the thought of seeing a part of you in another being."

"Yes, that's it exactly. I so long for a child. . . ."

Mara nodded. "After Clay and I got married, it was all I thought of. After waiting so long for a child, I finally told God I would be content with just Beth. I truly thought I couldn't have a baby." Her blue eyes brightened, and Emily thought they must rival the clear sky at the moment. "But look at me now. It'll happen for you too, Emily, I just know it."

Emily felt her jaw go slack then snap back in place. It couldn't possibly happen for her. Cade had seen to that. Her heart squeezed tight as if gripped by a vise.

"I'm sorry, I didn't mean to upset you."

Suddenly, the deep longing and disappointment welled up within her until she felt she would explode if she didn't give the feelings release. She tried to push back the feelings, and a knot formed in her throat.

Mara's hand settled on her arm. "What is it, Emily?"

Her throat worked, trying dislodge the lump, but it was going nowhere. And neither were these stubborn longings of hers. "I—" She tested Mara's expression with a glance then plunged ahead. "Cade and I won't be having children. We—we're husband and wife in name only." Her flesh grew warm at the confession. She remembered their wedding night and the way he'd rejected her.

"Oh, Emily, I didn't know."

She gave a dry laugh. "Neither did I." Next thing she knew, she was spilling the whole story starting with Cade's proposal on the stage and ending with his continued distance from her. Part of her wanted to tell Mara about the gold and her uncle's threat on her grandmother, but she was too ashamed. Besides, it was hard enough just sharing her humiliation about Cade.

"Do you have feelings for him?" Mara asked.

Emily fidgeted with her skirts, wondering if she could admit the fullness of her feelings for her husband. One glance at Mara's face convinced her she could. "I think I'm falling in love with him."

Mara squeezed her arm. "That's wonderful."

"No it's not." Her throat constricted. "He doesn't return my feelings, and I'm so weary of hiding mine from him."

"How do you know he doesn't feel the same?"

"He—he's distant with me, as if he doesn't want there to be anything between us. It's like he holds a shield in front of himself every time he's near me. I think he's still in love with Ingrid."

Mara looked away, her gaze moving off to some distant place.

"Did you know her? Ingrid?"

Mara nodded. "I got to know her a bit while she was carrying Adam. Just before she passed on. He did love her,

Emily, but it's been five years now. That's a long time to be without love, especially when he's had a son to raise alone."

Her heart twisted as she thought of Cade loving Ingrid. She longed for him to feel that way about her. "Well, he's not raising Adam alone anymore." She watched the boy shoot a marble through the dirt. Beth squealed and patted him on the shoulder.

"That's not right," Mara said. "You're taking care of Adam and the house for Cade, yet you've sacrificed your heart's desire."

Emily was starting to wonder exactly what her biggest heart's desire was: a child of her own or her husband's love. She wondered if she'd ever have either.

❧

Emily wiped her face with the back of her hand and knew she'd only smudged the dirt that coated her skin. She sat back on her haunches.

The lantern light flickered against the cave walls, casting eerie shadows on the dirt floor. Behind her, Adam dug for his own treasure in the dirt. She looked at the hole she'd spent the last hour digging and felt a surge of hopelessness. It was as empty as the last dozen holes she'd dug in this endless cavern of tunnels and halls. Who would have guessed that the little opening in the cliff wall would have so many corridors and rooms? Her back ached from stooping under low ceilings, her arms ached from digging in the packed earth.

She rubbed her neck and decided to call it a day. They would both need to get cleaned up, and she needed to get supper on before Cade got home.

After helping Adam find the remainder of his marbles, she grabbed the lantern from the stone ledge and began walking. Behind her, Adam's marbles clattered together in his pockets.

"I'm thirsty, Ma."

Even through her weariness, she smiled at the word. "Here, Sweetie." She handed him the canteen and waited while he drank. The coolness of the cave felt good against her warm flesh.

They continued until they came to a fork. She turned right. When they came to the next fork, she turned left.

"What's for supper? I'm starved."

She thought about the contents of their pantry. "How about beans and ham?"

As they wound through the cavern, they talked about all Adam's favorite meals. Emily was laughing at his description of zucchini when her gaze fell on the wall up ahead. Her heart stopped. She held the lantern up as the wall came into the fringe of light. A dead end.

Her heart jumped back to life even as her mouth dried up.

Adam bumped into her then wrapped an arm around her leg. "Why we stopping?"

Why was there a wall here? There was supposed to be another fork that would take them to the cave's entrance. She turned around and looked back where they'd come from. She must've taken a wrong turn.

"Let's go back this way."

When they reached the last fork, she turned left, hoping it would set them back on track. But at the end of that corridor, there were three tunnels branching off in the darkness.

I think we're lost, Lord.

"Which way, Ma?"

Which way? Which way? What if she couldn't find the way? What if they wandered around this cavern until their lamp flickered out for good?

Oh, help me, dear God.

nine

"Emily?" Cade wandered into the kitchen and dried his hands on a towel hanging from a hook. "Adam?" He glanced out the window toward the garden where bright green plants sprung up from the soil. Except for the leaves quivering in the wind, there was no movement there.

Where could they be? Normally, Adam barreled over to him before he got his horse put up for the night. Today, he was nowhere to be seen. Cade opened the oven door. Cold, gray ashes lay in a heap. She didn't even have a fire on for supper. He closed the oven door and walked to the foot of the stairs, scratching his stubbly chin.

"Emily? Adam?" His words echoed off the walls, then silence.

Hmm. Where could they be? He paced across the room, hunger clawing at his stomach. She always had supper on when he got home—usually had it on the table. Except the one time when he'd found her in the attic.

His stomach did a hard flop at the thought, and he told himself it was hunger. *Maybe she's in the attic again.* He trotted up the stairs and to the attic door, but it was closed. When he opened it, the pitch-black emptiness greeted him.

Where could they be? Had they run into town for something? He tried to remember if the wagon had been in its place when he'd put away Sutter. His mind had been elsewhere, and he couldn't be sure.

He went out to look. When he opened the barn door, the wagon sat off to his left in its usual spot. Sutter stirred in the hay, and Cade went to rub his nose. "Now where'd they take off to, boy, huh?"

Sutter nudged his nose up in the air and neighed.

That's when Cade noticed. Bitsy's stall was empty. "Now, how'd I miss that?" He walked over to the empty stall as if it would give him some clue where Emily went. "Huh."

He heaved a sigh and went back into the house. After waiting awhile, he gave in to his hunger and slathered a piece of bread with marmalade. Had she gone to the mercantile for something? Or over to Mara's?

He chawed on the bread, his mind beginning to wander off to places he didn't want it to go. What if they'd fallen from Bitsy, and Emily or Adam was injured? What if Emily were hurt, and they were too far from home for Adam to get help? What if Adam were trying to find his way and had gotten lost?

Stop it, Manning. They'd probably just lost track of time, that's all. Like she had that day in the attic. He scooted back his chair and brushed the crumbs from his lap. They were fine. It wasn't that late.

An hour later, he walked out to the porch, peering out into the growing darkness. He could still make out the silhouette of trees and hills, but soon the night would cover the land like a heavy shroud. If Emily or Adam were lost, they would never find their way in the dark.

His feet beat a path to the barn. He had to do something. Enough of this sitting around and waiting. He couldn't take it any longer. Once inside the barn, he grabbed the tack and headed to Sutter's stall. The horse blinked lazy eyes his way.

Where would he go once he got saddled up? To Mara and Clay's house? She couldn't be there. If she'd lost track of time, it surely would have dawned on her when Clay arrived home for supper. The mercantile was closed, so she couldn't be there.

Where is she, Lord? Keep them safe. The thought of Adam hurt or worse twisted his gut. Fear sucked the moisture from his throat, and his heart quivered in his chest. *Calm down, it's going to be all right.*

But memories of another night assaulted him. Another night when he'd thought everything was going to be all right. And that night had ended with a dead wife.

Blinded by worry, Cade opened the stall door and tossed the saddle blanket over Sutter's back. As he smoothed the blanket flat and saddled her up, his mind played cruel tricks. What if he found them dead somewhere? Ingrid's still form flashed in his mind, and his limbs grew cold. He couldn't lose Adam, he couldn't.

And Emily. The thought of something happening to her made his heart hurt. He didn't know where he would look, but something had happened or Emily would have brought them home. He would search all night if he had to. Maybe he should go to Clay and Mara's house first and get some help.

He heard the noise just as he pulled Sutter from the stall. He stopped, going still to listen. Hoofbeats. His heart gave a jump of hope. He left Sutter and trotted to the barn door.

Darkness had swallowed the yard, and the only light came from the lantern he'd lit in the barn. His gaze detected a shadowed movement, and he focused on that spot until the object moved into the circle of light.

His breath left his body in a sudden gush. Bitsy sauntered

toward him, Emily and Adam perched on her back. He searched their bodies for any sign of injury, but found no evidence. Even in the dim light, he could see they were both coated with filth.

When Emily noticed him, her eyes widened, then her chin tipped down.

"Pa!" Adam's weary shoulders straightened, and he held out his arms for Cade.

When Bitsy stopped, Cade pulled his son into his arms, holding him tighter than necessary. *Thank You, Jesus.* "Are you all right? Are you hurt?"

"Nuh-uh. We got lost in the cave, and it was dark!"

Cade's gaze found Emily, but her gaze was averted. "A cave?"

"We were looking for treasure!" Adam said.

Emily's gaze darted to his this time, and he studied her face.

Adam dug into his pocket and pulled out some marbles. "And I found 'em all again, didn't I, Ma?"

As the relief drained away, something rose up in its place. Something deep and unsettling. She'd taken his boy on some foolhardy treasure hunt and gotten them lost so he could fret for hours? So he could sit around and worry that they were hurt or—or dead? It was dark and late, and who knows what could have happened to them, traipsing around the country-side all alone?

Heat coursed through his veins, penetrating his limbs. He narrowed his gaze on Emily. "You'd best get inside and get your-self cleaned up." His voice grated across his throat. What he'd like to do is put her over his lap and give her a sound whipping.

She clambered down from the horse and pulled Adam

from his arms. When Cade set him on the ground, she whisked him off for a bath.

By the time a simple supper was on the table, Cade was too angry to eat. Did she have any idea the fright she'd given him? He glanced at her over his glass of lemonade. She'd hardly spoken two words all through the meal. But then she didn't need to with Adam here. The more details the boy gave about their little outing, the more he wanted to give Emily what for.

She met his gaze then, and he gave her a look that promised a heated discussion later.

≈

Emily eyed Cade across from her, the ache in her stomach spreading outward and filling her with dread. Her relief at finding their way out of the cave had only lasted as long as it had taken to arrive home. Once she'd seen the worry and anger on Cade's face, she'd known she was in for a dressing-down.

"Get on upstairs and get ready for bed," Cade told his son.

Obediently, Adam wiped his mouth then trotted up the stairs.

Cade's chair scraped loudly across the plank floor, and Emily jumped.

Without a word, he left the table, and Emily began gathering up the dirty dishes.

She drew in a deep breath, exhaling loudly. She was plumb tuckered from the long day. Putting in chores, then searching for the gold, then getting lost. . . She smothered a yawn. Just before the lantern had flickered out, she'd seen the cave opening with the moonlight streaming in. If the light had gone out earlier, she and Adam might still be lost in the belly of the cave. She shuddered at the thought. After tonight, the thought of going back into the dank cave was more than she could bear. She could still smell the stale moisture of the rock walls, still feel them closing in on her.

The floor creaked above her head, and her stomach twisted. Cade was waiting until he had her alone to confront her. He hadn't had to tell her that; it was plain in the look he'd given her.

She dried off the last plate, hung the towel to dry, and dumped the dirty water.

She passed Cade on the stairs as she went up to bid Adam good night. He avoided her gaze, and her heart sunk. She was dreading the confrontation. She was guilty, after all, of causing him worry. And what if he'd become suspicious? What else had Adam told him about their adventure today? Would Cade believe she'd taken Adam there solely as a diversion for him?

In Adam's room, she sat on the edge of his bed and told him a story she made up as she went along. The story grew so long, she realized she was stalling. Finally, she tacked on an appropriate ending and smiled as Adam clapped with glee.

After kissing the boy on the cheek and ruffling his dark hair, Emily blew out the flame in the lantern and pulled his door shut.

She turned and faced the stairs with equal measures of dread and resolve. *Might as well get this over with.*

He was waiting for her by the hearth when she entered the room. He turned, his face a mask of anger, his hand grasping the rough-hewn mantel.

He wasted no time with trivialities. "Do you have any notion of the worry you caused me tonight?"

She opened her mouth, but he wasn't finished.

"At first I thought you'd just lost track of time. But when it started getting dark and you still weren't back, that's when I really fretted."

He crossed his arms over his broad chest.

Her legs quaked under her and she sank onto the couch, hating the way he now towered over her.

"What do you think you were doing in that cave? What if you hadn't found your way out? What if it had collapsed on you—those things happen, you know. Or maybe you don't know. Maybe you just went on your frivolous adventure all willy-nilly, never mind the chores that were waiting or the dangers of the cave, you took my son, my son, and risked his life."

"I'm sorry, I—"

Cade continued, mentioning dangers of caves she hadn't even known existed. Her gaze clung to her skirts like a cat clinging to a tree. He was right, she knew that now. She never should have taken Adam into the cave. She wouldn't have, if only she'd been aware of the risks. Still, it had been an innocent mistake.

"And it was irresponsible. If you can't take care of him proper-like, maybe I need to find someone else." He turned toward the fireplace, but she heard him muttering, "Gallivanting all over the countryside. . ."

If you can't take care of him proper-like. A bubble of heat welled up in her stomach. Hadn't she taken good care of Adam for weeks now? Hadn't she loved him like her own son? She'd taught him, played with him, nurtured him, and now he was accusing her of being a neglectful mother?

He continued muttering to the mantel. "A mistake all along. Should've sent her packing that day."

Deep within her, the rolling heat gave birth to an inferno. How dare he criticize her when she'd kept her end of the bargain! She'd cared for his son, done all the daily chores, cooked his meals, washed his clothes, cleaned up his messes, and what had she gotten in return? Nothing, that's what! She'd made all the sacrifices; he'd gained all the privileges, just like Mara had said. He had gotten all he wanted from her yet he had denied her the desire of her heart. He had denied her children.

"How dare you." Her voice sounded deep and harsh in the quiet of the room. Somehow, she'd come to her feet.

"I have cared for Adam like he was my own. Don't you dare say I have neglected that child." Her eyes stung with the fervency of her feelings for Adam. "I made a mistake today. A mistake. Am I not entitled to one every now and again?" Her voice quivered as it grew louder. "But I would never do anything to endanger that child.

"I have done nothing but wait on you, hand and foot. I have washed your clothes, cooked your food, mended your garments. . . ." She picked up the sewing basket and threw it at his feet.

His expression was laced with surprise, though his planted feet didn't budge.

"And what have I gotten in return? You have denied me the joy of ever holding my own child in my arms. Never mind that you didn't even tell me this before I married you! And now I'll never have a child of my own, never!" He blurred in front of her, and she knew her eyes had filled with tears. Her throat ached, and her stomach felt hollow. She turned from him, crossing her arms, feeling suddenly exposed and strangely relieved. It was all true, and why shouldn't he know it? He was being selfish and cruel.

She didn't know he stood behind her until she felt him touch her shoulder.

Every muscle in her body tensed. His touch was gentle yet strong, and she hated the way it made her heart lurch.

"I'm sorry," he said.

His voice sounded in her ear, and suddenly she realized how close he was. She could feel the heat of his body.

"I lost my temper. I shouldn't have said what I did."

As he spoke, the curls on her nape whispered softly against her skin, sending gooseflesh up and down her arms.

"You never told me about wanting a child."

It was true, she hadn't. But didn't every woman want children? He should have known.

His hand squeezed the flesh of her arm, and heat kindled there. "I wasn't thinking straight that day on the stage. All those people watching. . . I just didn't know how to say it."

Her lips trembled, and she put a hand against them.

He turned her around and her heart caught. His broad chest was inches from her face, and she focused on one of the pearly buttons on his shirt. She couldn't bring herself to meet his gaze, though she felt it as sure as a touch. She closed her eyes, then felt his hand on her chin, tipping it up.

When she opened her eyes, his gaze burned into hers, and her legs trembled under her. His eyes darkened to a deep bluish green. Their depths held a mix of sorrow and something else she was afraid to define. His thumb moved along her jaw, blazing a trail of fire. Her heart threatened to escape her chest. She closed her eyes again lest he see the depth of her feelings.

ten

His thumb traced the curve of her lip, and she thought she'd surely faint dead away. Why was he doing this? It was sweet torture.

There were no words, and no world around them, just the touch of his hand and the fire of his gaze. Though she'd never been kissed, she knew this man, her husband, wanted to kiss her now. And she longed for it with all her heart.

He leaned closer until she could see the tiny flecks of color in his eyes. She wanted to drown in their depths, but more than that, she wanted to feel his lips on hers. Even now, she felt the heat of his breath caress her lips.

"Ma?" Adam's voice echoed down the stairs.

She froze in place, as did Cade, and her heart beat out an emphatic complaint.

"Pa?"

Cade's hands fell to his side, and the flesh they'd left went suddenly cold.

His gaze flitted over hers, and she read the reluctance in them. He walked to the stairs and spoke from there. "What is it?" His voice sounded raspy and mildly irritated. Was he as disappointed as she at having been interrupted?

"I got a question 'bout heaven."

Cade tossed her a look, and she suddenly felt silly standing alone in the middle of the room.

Before she could move, he went up the stairs. The moment

was gone, and she feared there would never be another like it.

That night, she pulled out her diary from its secret spot and put her thoughts on paper.

Dear Diary,

I feel compelled to broach a subject I have avoided all these weeks here in Cedar Springs. It's silly of me, but somehow I felt if I didn't write my feelings in these pages, they would just disappear. I'm speaking of my feelings for my husband.

Such a whirlwind of emotions are even now flooding my mind. Moments ago, I was so angry with him I could have screamed.

I have never seen him angry like he was tonight, and as much as it distressed me, I realize how different his anger was from Uncle Stewart's. I had no fear tonight of harm coming to my own person. Still, his anger bothered me in a different way. I think it's because I care so much what he thinks of me. And to think that he was disappointed in me was most distressing.

But I couldn't let him think as badly of me as he did. In his anger, he'd said things that weren't justified, hence my own temper flared. But somehow, just a kind word and a touch from him, and I was pliable as dough.

My face heats as I write this, but, Diary, tonight he nearly kissed me. My heart has still not recovered, nor has my deep disappointment that we were interrupted before his lips met mine. Has another woman ever felt so overwhelmed at her husband's touch? I wonder if it's inappropriate to feel so much desire.

Well, these questions won't be answered tonight, and

right now, I long to curl up on my bed and dream
sweet dreams.

❧

Cade pulled his chair back with a scrape and let his weary body fall onto it. He could hear Emily at the stove scraping breakfast from the skillet. Next to him, Adam rested his chubby cheek against his palm, his eyes closed against the morning.

Cade rubbed his own eyes. Sleep had been slow in coming last night on account of his confused thoughts. By the time he'd answered all Adam's questions about heaven and hell, Emily had gone to bed. A part of him had been relieved, but another part was disappointed. He'd wanted to kiss her, no denying that. He was starting to cotton to her, and there was no denying that either.

He picked up the pitcher and filled their cups with fresh milk.

Was it so wrong of him to want his new wife? To have feelings for her? Those were the questions that had kept him awake for the better part of the night. The kitchen door creaked open, and Emily appeared, a basket of biscuits in her hand. He rose and took it from her, setting it square on the table, and she turned back to the kitchen.

He watched her go, her calico skirts swinging in rhythm with her steps. He admired the way the material clung to her narrow waist then flowed out from the flare of her hips.

Heat flooded his face at the direction of his thoughts. All last night, he'd seen her face behind his closed eyes. Her deep brown eyes and cherry lips that trembled with anger. He'd come so close to kissing them. Would they have softened under his ministrations?

Emily came through the door, this time holding a platter filled with ham and eggs. He rose briefly until she settled into her seat, then he said grace.

She scooped some eggs onto Adam's plate while he speared a slab of ham.

She had yet to meet his gaze, and he knew she felt just as awkward about their embrace as he did. As they ate the meal, the strain was thick. Only Adam spoke, finally wakened by the tasty food in his belly.

"We going to the cave again today?"

The question was directed at Emily, but the answer slipped from Cade's mouth before he could stop it. "No."

Adam turned to him with an argument on his lips, but Cade put a stop to it. "You're not allowed going into the caves again. It's not safe."

"But me and Emily—"

"Answer's no, and that's final. I'll not hear another word about it, understand?"

His son's eyes flashed blue then his gaze fell away. "Yes sir."

Cade looked at Emily, but she studied the eggs on her plate as she moved them around with her fork.

Even Adam fell silent after that, and Cade wondered if Emily was thinking that he didn't trust her. He remembered her emphatic words from the night before and how he'd hurt her feelings. He still felt bad about that, even after apologizing. He hoped she understood about the caves.

His gaze darted her way just in time to catch hers. They held for a memorable moment.

With a loud clank, Adam's glass turned over and milk flowed across the table. Emily got up for a towel, and the moment was broken again.

❧

All that afternoon, Cade couldn't get Emily from his mind. He hadn't been without a woman for so long that he didn't recognize the feelings that had been building in him. Emily was no longer a mere boarder in his home. She was no longer just a fill-in mother for his son. She was coming to be special to him. A part of his heart, a part he'd thought long dead, was coming alive again. And as much as that scared him, it excited him too. He wondered what his brother would have thought of this? *Would Thomas approve of my feelings for Emily?*

He nodded thoughtfully and pulled Sutter's reins until he stopped. Thomas would approve. He probably would've thumped Cade on the forehead for being stubborn about it so long.

He led the horse to the creek and let him drink his fill, then squatted beside him and filled his canteen. As the clear water rushed into the small opening, Cade knew he'd made a decision he wouldn't go back on. He would pursue this relationship with Emily. Slowly, carefully, he would try to win the heart of his son's mother—his wife.

❧

Emily picked up the yellow yarn and started working on what was going to be a blanket for Mara's baby. She'd settled on the most delicate colors and though she'd barely started, she knew it was going to be the perfect gift.

Upstairs, the floor creaked where Cade no doubt stood beside Adam's bed. His announcement over breakfast that she wasn't to take Adam into caves had left her reeling. What was she going to do now? How would she search for the gold and obey Cade's wishes? She couldn't leave the boy at home or even at the cave's entrance all alone. He was too young to stay out of trouble, and she would never forgive herself if something happened to him. Cade was right. A cave was no place for a child. But that left her in a quandary. The only person whom she knew well enough to ask for help was Mara, but what reason could she give to her friend why she needed help with Adam so often? She couldn't bring herself to lie. All the deceptions with her husband were a heavy enough burden. She couldn't sully her relationship with her only real friend.

And perhaps if she gave up the search, her relationship with her husband would improve. Cade had cast strange glances her way during both breakfast and supper until she wanted to set down her utensils and ask him if she had pre-serves on her chin. And over supper, he'd talked to her. To her, not just to Adam. He'd asked her about the garden and told her he'd chop more wood for the stove. And besides that, he'd looked at her when he'd spoken.

Her insides got all quivery just thinking about it. She looked at the spot across the room where they'd stood together last night—and she'd lost her temper in a way she had never done. She'd given him a good dressing-down for his ingratitude, and now she felt bad about it. She could hardly believe she'd bared her soul that way, told him of her disappointment. Now he knew how badly she wanted young 'uns.

That's it. He's being kindly toward me because he feels guilty. A lump of disappointment formed in her stomach. *He feels sorry for me.* Only when she felt the keen stab of regret did she realize she'd been hoping for something else. She'd been hoping all day that he was growing fond of her.

Did he embrace her the night before because he pitied

her? Because he felt bad that he'd ruined her dream of having children? Her face flooded with heat, and she was glad he was upstairs at the moment.

Lord, this marriage is a mess, she prayed. *I'm so confused by Cade's behavior, Father, and I'm so tired of hiding my feelings from him.*

The creaks on the stairs alerted her to Cade's entrance. She pretended to be absorbed in her knitting, but every nerve in her body was aware of his presence, of his movement across the room. He settled in his chair in the corner by the fireplace.

"Adam's all tucked away for the night."

The needles trembled in her hands, clacking together. "Good." Was her voice as wobbly as she thought? Why wasn't he picking up his Bible from the mantel? Why was he just sitting there? She could feel his gaze on her.

"He said you went to town today."

From the corner of her eye, she could see him cross his legs. "Picked up some yarn for this blanket."

"Clay told me they were expecting."

Her skin prickled with heat, and she wondered if her face bloomed with color. Why had she mentioned the baby blanket? Now he must be thinking of her words last night.

"Corn's coming up good. Old man Owens said he thought this might be the best crop in years, barring a drought."

"That's good." Why couldn't she think of anything else to say? He must think her addlepated.

"If we get a good price on it, I was thinking to build on a water closet on the east side of the house."

She glanced at him then back to her work. How wonderful it would be to have a necessity! Especially in the cold of winter.

"Parnell said he could get me good price on one of those bathtubs too."

"A bathtub? Really?" Oh, how nice it would be not to haul water to the stove and heat it up for each bath.

His eyes sparkled in the lantern light. "If we have a good crop."

She worked her needles, and they clicked together breaking the silence. Finally, Cade retrieved his Bible from the mantel and settled in the chair. As she knitted, her mind spun. Was he offering to build the necessity out of kindness to her? Men didn't care about such things did they? Her heart skittered in her chest. Would he do that for her?

Even as she worked, she could feel his gaze on hers, but she couldn't bring herself to meet it. Either he was feeling sorry for her or he was growing fond of her, and she couldn't bear to expose her feelings until she knew for sure one way or the other.

eleven

Dear Uncle Stewart,
 *I hope this letter finds you and Nana well. I'm finding
the life of a farmer's wife is both exhausting and rewarding.*

Emily leaned back and read the lines. Her uncle had a dis-liking for small talk, but the next words she wrote must be exactly right. *Help me say this in a way he'll accept, Lord. I'm so tired of this awful game, of deceiving Cade. Let this be the end of it, please.*

 *I'm afraid I have some bad news. Last week Adam
and I became lost in one of the caves while I was search-ing. It's only by God's grace that we found our way out.
The caves here seem endless with many tunnels leading
in many directions. One could disappear into one of
them and never come out alive. I have spent many hours
searching that particular cave to no avail. There are so
many places the gold could be hidden, and no way of
knowing where it is. There are several other caves in the
area where the gold could also be buried. I could search
for years and never find it.*
 *In addition to that, I have found it's very dangerous
work. Caves can collapse, leaving a person buried alive.
Wild animals are known to make their homes in these
caves. And, as I recently discovered, one can become*

hopelessly lost. In all honesty, I cannot risk Adam's
well-being by taking him into these hazardous caverns
anymore. After last week's disaster, his father has for-
bidden it anyway. Because of these safety reasons and
because of the hopelessness of ever finding what you
seek, I think it would be best to discontinue the search.
Please be reasonable about this, Uncle. I know you are
displeased to hear this, but please know that I have
given it my best effort.

    *You needn't be burdened with Nana any longer. I would
love to take care of her here if you will only send her to me.
I will gladly pay her fare, and you will not have to care for
her anymore. Please write soon. Until then, know that I
care for you and am praying for you both.*

Love,
Emily

She sighed and covered her mouth with a trembling hand.
Would her uncle accept her words? *Please, Lord, help Uncle
Stewart be fair-minded.* What other hope had she?

    ❦

"Did you know my mama?" Adam asked.

His question stilled the breath in Emily's body. Her hands,
too, stilled on the lump of dough before they resumed their
kneading. "No, I didn't. I know she was very special, though,
and that she loved you very much."

Adam squished the small wad of dough she'd given him to
play with. "She died when I was borned."

"I know." She wished she knew what else to say. Was the
boy missing his real ma? The thought brought an ache to her
own stomach. She'd grown to think of him as her own son.

Something had happened once she'd written that letter to her uncle. It was as if it had freed her. There was no wall of lies between her and her husband and no tricking Adam into going on treasure hunts. Somehow it seemed she was truly his mother now and not just playing a role.

"Pa said she's in heaven." He flattened the dough.

"Sure enough. She had Jesus in her heart just like you." Emily smiled down at him, but when she saw his wide blue eyes gloss over with tears, her heart caught.

She knelt down and put her hand on his arm, mindless of the sticky flour that coated it. "Oh, Sweetheart. What is it?"

His chin quivered, and a tiny frown puckered between his brows. "What if you go away too?" His eyes scrunched up, and he dove into her arms.

She embraced him, her own eyes stinging. He was worried he was going to lose her like he had lost his ma. She remembered when her own mother had died. Consumption, they'd said, but it had seemed so unfair. At least she'd known her ma. Adam had never gotten that chance.

"I can't promise that bad things won't happen, Adam. But God has it all under control, and He has a purpose in everything He does."

She pulled back and looked him in the eye. "Why, just look at us. Didn't God bring you into my life? What would I do without my special boy?" Her throat ached with a knot that seemed lodged there. "And you needed a mama, and didn't God send me to you? You see, He cares for us and provides for us." She smiled through her own tears and wiped Adam's cheeks. Flour from her hands dusted his face. She chuckled. "You've got flour on your face now."

A smile wobbled on his lips, and he put a powdered finger on her nose. "Got you back."

She laughed and hugged him tight, her love for him welling up in her.

"I love you, Ma."

Warmth enveloped her like a thick, cozy quilt. "I love you too, Son." And she realized then that she truly did love this child of her heart the way she would love a child of her body.

※

"Look, Ma, a matatoe!"

Emily looked up from the straggly weed she'd gripped and laughed. "Sure enough, it's a tomato."

"Can I pick it?"

"Oh, no, not yet. See how green it is? It won't do for cooking until it's red as a cherry." She yanked with all her might, and the weed came uprooted. "You keep an eye on it, though. It'll be red before we know it."

The garden was coming along nicely, and she took pride in the plants she'd tended so carefully. Come winter, they'd have a cellar full of vegetables to last through the cold months. She'd have a lot of canning to do.

In the two weeks since she'd written to her uncle, she'd felt like a whole new woman. Though she was anxious to hear from him, she felt sure he would come to his senses. *He should know it's futile, and he's surely eager to be rid of Nana.*

She would have to broach the subject with Cade soon. It wouldn't be too hard given the way he'd taken to talking to her. Twice now, he'd even touched her shoulder as he passed by in a way that had made her skin heat and her heart sigh. In church last Sunday, he'd put his arm across the pew behind her shoulders, and she scarcely understood a word Reverend Hill uttered from that point on.

Is he really starting to care for me, Lord? It seemed so impossible that he would, but wasn't God capable of anything? Even changing the heart of her stubborn husband?

Having not heard Adam making any noise, she glanced up to see what he was up to. He was splayed out on his belly in front of the same tomato plant, his gaze fixed earnestly on the green vegetable.

A smile tilted her lips, and she sat back on her haunches. "Adam, what are you doing?"

He spared her a glance. "Keeping an eye on the matatoe."

"But why?"

"You said it'd turn red soon."

Emily chuckled, delighted at his earnestness. She scooted over beside him and tickled his belly. "I'll bet I can make you turn red sooner."

He laughed and rolled away, but she crawled after him on her knees. "Gotcha!" She sprinkled his ribs and knees with tickles, and he laughed until his face colored. Before she knew it, she was lying in the dirt beside him, a tomato plant crowding over her shoulder.

"Well now." The voice from the edge of the garden made her shoot upright. Cade stood there, silhouetted by the sun. His hands rested on his hips. "I think I see a couple nuts ripe for pickin'."

Adam jumped up beside her. "Pa!" He ran across down the row of plants, leaving footprints behind him. "We didn't plant no nuts."

As Cade swung Adam into his arms, Emily stood and dusted the dirt from her skirts.

"Is it that late?" she asked. The sun was behind the house, but it seemed too early for Cade to come home. Was he angry she'd been fooling around instead of working? *Why does he always seem to catch me at the worst possible moment?*

"Nah, came home early today. Thought I might know a young 'un that'd like to go wading in the creek."

Adam squealed and squirmed until Cade set him down.

Emily walked toward them feeling a bit out of place. Her bonnet had slipped off and hung from the ribbons tied at her neck. She felt her hair and tried to tuck away the damp strands that had come loose.

"Will you teach me to swim, Pa? Please?"

"Not tonight. Thought we'd go to that shallow spot by Bender's Meadow."

Emily turned toward the house. She supposed she could get the floor mopped up while they were gone. Hearing the happy chitchat behind her made her feel strangely empty inside. She felt like a fifth wheel. Cade and his son were a pair. Where did she belong?

While Cade went to hitch up the wagon, Emily filled the tin pail with water from the pump and shaved some soap into it. She looked across the length of the house and felt a sigh well up in her. *No use moaning about it, Emily Jane, it needs to be done.*

As she dipped the mop into the water, Cade entered the house.

"What are you doing?"

She pulled the sopping mop from the water. "Mopping the floor."

His expression seemed to fall, and she wondered what she'd done now.

He tapped his hat against his thigh, his gaze scanning the floor. "You don't want to come along?"

Her heart sailed high at his words. He'd assumed she would come with them.

"I thought you might pack us a little supper, and we'd picnic alongside the creek. If you want to, I mean."

Her hands tightened on the mop handle, the soppy weight of it bearing down on her arms. A picnic. She felt a smile tugging on her lips. "That sounds just fine. Let me just. . ." She looked back toward the kitchen, wondering what she'd fix for their picnic, but turned back, realizing she still had a mop in her hands.

"Here, let me get that." Cade took the mop from her hands and picked up the full bucket. "Something quick and easy's just fine."

She nodded and scurried off to pack the meal.

❧

Before long, they were at the bend in the creek. She selected a spot on the high bank under a weeping willow tree, its graceful branches hanging down around them like a veil. Adam slipped off his shoes and stockings and slid down the grassy incline.

"Careful you don't fall," she called.

While Cade gathered the basket from the wagon, she spread the colorful quilt over the grass and sank down in the cool shade. She slid off her bonnet, and the evening breeze ruffled the stray hairs. She patted it, wishing she'd taken the time to put it up again. The knot was loose, and some of the pins were sliding out.

Cade set the basket beside her. "You should take it down, now that it's cooling off."

She lowered her hands, and heat crawled up her neck at having been caught primping.

"Come on, Pa!" Adam called from the edge of the creek. Sunlight broke through the leafy canopy and kissed the water here and there with splotches of light.

"Comin'," Cade called. He tugged off his boots and socks and began rolling up the ends of trousers. His calves were thick with muscle and covered with hair as black as the ones on his head.

"You coming in?" Cade's gaze was fixed on her, his lips tilted in a crooked grin, his eyes sparkling with amusement.

He'd caught her staring! She began unpacking the basket. "I'll just stay here and get everything ready."

In the fringes of her vision, she saw him stand to his feet. "Suit yourself."

It didn't take long to set out the simple fixin's of bread, apples, and cheese. Once she did, she watched Adam and Cade playing together in the water, reluctant to interrupt.

When they walked downstream a ways, she laid back against the soft, worn quilt and closed her eyes. She could hear a bird chirping in a tree above her, and the wind sighing through the leaves. She drew in a breath and let the day's worries and frustrations slide away. The last thing she remembered hearing was a squirrel chattering off in the distance.

A faint tickling sensation on her nose tugged her from someplace warm and lazy. She brushed at her nose, drifting away once again.

Again, something tickled her nose, and she reached up to swat it away. She gradually became aware of a cricket chirping somewhere nearby. Her eyes opened. Above her, Cade's face hovered, and she could feel the heat from his body so near her own. She looked around.

The picnic. I fell asleep. "Adam." She started to sit up, but Cade put a hand on her shoulder.

"He's fine. Just trying to catch tadpoles."

She noticed the willow twig in his hand, its feathery leaves dangling down toward her stomach. "You were tickling me."

His smile made her heart skip a beat. "Guilty." But he didn't look guilty at all. In fact, he looked completely unrepentant. His jaw was shadowed with a day's worth of stubble, and she thought for the first time that it only added to his rugged good looks.

"Shame on you," she said, studying for the first time the way the sun had tanned his skin, leaving only fine white lines bursting around the corners of his eyes.

"You're pretty when you're sleeping."

"Only when I'm sleeping?" *Did I just say that?* She sat up and felt the heavy mane of hair fall onto her back. The pins had finally come loose. In her hair and her brain.

She didn't know how close she was to Cade until she felt the whisper of his breath across her face. "No," he said.

She looked him in the eye, and her heart stilled at his nearness. "What?"

"You're right pretty all the time."

He picked up a length of her dark hair and ran it between his fingers. Chills shot down her neck and across her arm.

"I'm hungry!" Adam called.

She turned to see him running up the incline, his britches wet and soggy and splotches of darkness flecking his shirt.

"I caught me a tadpole, Ma!"

She gathered her wits. "Where is it?"

"Got away. We eating soon?"

Emily busied herself smoothing out the blanket. When she reached Cade's corner, he remained unmoved, staring at her, a smile on his face that would melt ice. She moved to the center where Adam sat with a plate already filled with the picnic fixin's.

After they filled their bellies, Emily packed the basket and blanket while Cade untied the horses. The ride back seemed longer somehow than the ride here, but perhaps it was only because Adam was not separating them this time. Cade's thick thigh rubbed up alongside hers until she could think of little else.

By the time they'd arrived back at the farm, the sun had sunk from the sky, leaving only a sliver of moonlight to see by. Cade lifted Adam down from the wagon and handed him the basket and blanket. "Think you can carry all that?"

"Yes, Sir!" Adam swaggered into the house, clearly pleased to be a helper.

Cade turned then and gave her a hand down. His hand felt large and warm in hers. It would have been comforting if not for the way it set her heart to racing. She turned to the house.

"Stay out here awhile."

She turned to look at him.

"Light a lantern for me?" he asked.

She moved into the barn where the lantern hung on a peg and lit it. She turned and watched as he unhitched the horses with sure, strong movements. He was an enigma, this man. This brother of her dear friend, Thomas. How she wished she'd had a brother or a father who'd been alive long enough for her to figure out how a man's mind worked. As it was, she was at a loss. Surely most men were nothing like Uncle Stewart.

One day Cade was like a stranger living in the same house,

and the next he's like a friend who wants to be my—

Her throat grew dry at the thought, and her traitorous heart beat a jig she was sure Reverend Hill would disapprove of. *You're being silly, Emily. He's just a man. He only wanted you to light the lantern, and here you stand staring after him like a forlorn schoolmarm at a barn dance. Why he'd probably think you were daft if he even knew the directions of your—*

It was only then she'd noticed he was standing in front of her. Not just in front of her but *right* in front of her. Surely no more than a whistle away. The glow of light hit his face at all the right angles, kissing his upper cheekbones, letting shadows seep into the recesses of his jaw. His dark lashes had lowered to nearly his cheekbones, leaving just a sliver of those sparkling eyes in view. She'd give the baby quilt she'd worked on for weeks for just an inkling of what was going on behind them.

"I've been praying, Emily."

"Oh?" If her heart jumped any harder, surely it would bump his chest.

"You know, about us."

She nodded as if she knew what he was talking about. He'd long ago slid the hat from his head, and the dark strands of hair framed his face, the light glimmering off them.

"You've been a gift to Adam and me. A gift from God, and I got to wondering how He'd feel about how accepting I've been of that gift." He lowered his head, the shadows enshrouding his face. "I reckon it must look to God like I took the gift He gave me, put it on a shelf, and said 'no thanks.'"

Her face heated at his words. Her heart kept tempo with the music in her soul, and she held her breath waiting for the words she hoped to hear.

twelve

"Last night I told God 'thank You,' " Cade said. "He's sent me a wonderful mother for my son and a wonderful woman to be my wife." The flesh of his palm found her cheek, and his thumb rubbed across her lips until she thought her knees would give way.

"When we married, I didn't know you wanted young 'uns. Shoulda known, I guess, but I didn't give it much thought. I was too wrapped up in my own needs." His other hand found her face, and she felt wonderfully surrounded by the comfort of his flesh.

"What I'm trying to say, I suppose, is that I'd like to give this marriage a fighting chance—if you're willing, that is."

Eyes the color of a blue spruce questioned her in the glow of the lamplight. Her heart took flight at his words.

"I've come to care for you a great deal, Emily. I think we make a good match, you and I. And I'd like to. . .I'd like to court you the way a man courts a woman. I don't know much about you, but I want to learn everything. I want to know whether you wore hair ribbons as a girl and if some boy ever broke your heart. I want to know how you feel about moving here to Cedar Springs, and—I want to know if you could ever care for me."

His last sentence ended in a whisper she felt all the way to her toes. His lips, inches away, begged to be kissed. She looked deeply into his eyes, hoping he'd read her feelings there, because suddenly, not a word would squeak from her parched throat.

His lips lowered onto hers, slowly, maddeningly slowly. Her heart quickened, and she met his lips with a desperation born of loneliness and desire. His lips teased with soft brushes, tasting, testing, until she feared she'd go mad for want of him.

Finally, he embraced her, pulling her closer to him than she had ever been. Her skin heated up like a stoked bonfire. She wondered if her ears glowed orange with the warmth of it. His hands curved around the back of her head, holding her firmly, lovingly.

Her hands worked up his strong chest and rested there.

A moment later, he pulled away, though their arms still embraced one another. Their breathing came quickly. Cade's eyelids were half shut, a lazy surprise in his eyes.

She pulled away. She could hardly believe his effect on her. Weren't women supposed to be subdued and—well, they certainly weren't supposed to be so, so needy and eager! Her gaze found the hay-strewn floor even as heat crept up her neck. What must he think of her now? She'd behaved like a wanton woman instead of a wife doing her duty. She was still breathing heavily. Shameful!

She felt his knuckle tip up her chin. His lips tipped in a crooked smile, but she noticed he, too, had not yet caught his breath. "You are some woman, Emily Manning," he rasped.

She looked away. What had he meant by that? Had she shamed him as well as herself?

He stepped closer again, this time wrapping her up in his arms like a big, cozy quilt. He planted a kiss on her nose.

What was he thinking? Oh, that she could read his mind and have done with it.

He laid his cheek against hers. She shivered, and he wrapped his arms more tightly around her. "Stop fretting," he whispered in her ear. Then he took her hand and placed it against his heart. She could feel it beating under the plaid shirt, beating as fast as hers. What was he saying?

The answer came softly in her ear. "This is what you do to me, Emmie."

She smiled at the word her father used to call her.

"This is a good thing."

"I'm scared." *I can't believe I admitted that.*

His arms tightened. "It's all right. I am too."

He held her for several moments of bliss while their hearts settled back into a steady rhythm beneath their homespun clothes. He pulled away. "I reckon Adam must be wondering what's become of us."

She nodded, still dazed.

"Let's take it a day at a time, all right?"

She nodded again.

He drew her hands up to his mouth and laid his firm, soft lips against them. "All this is new to me too, you know. It's been so long. . . ."

Ha, she thought. *He could coax a bear from a honey hive!*

He curled his warm hand around hers, and together they went into the house to begin again.

❧

Several days later, Emily scraped the bacon grease from the pan while Adam dried off a plate. Behind her, Cade's chair grated across the wooden floor. She was ever so aware of him these days. He was like a cool breeze when he entered the room, and her skin shivered in his presence.

"I'm going to town this morning, be back in a few hours," he said over his shoulder.

She turned, but he was already through the doorway. She

dried off her hands and chased after him.

"Cade!"

He turned, that handsome, lopsided grin tilted on his face. Her heart flopped.

"What is it, Emmie?"

The nickname still made her tremble. "I was—I want to go with you if it's not too much trouble."

Was it her imagination, or did his smile widen a fraction?

He gave a nod. "I'll hitch up the bays while you finish the dishes."

She smiled. "All right." She watched him all the way to the barn, his long legs eating up the distance quickly, then returned to the kitchen.

Once the dishes were in order, she went to the pantry and picked up her real reason for going into town. Her marionberry preserves. She'd topped the lids with a circle of cloth and had tied thin ribbons around the necks of the jars. When Mrs. Parnell had bragged on her preserves at the church social and asked for a few jars for the mercantile, Emily had felt so proud. Now, maybe she'd be able to earn a few pennies of her own and please Cade too.

She packed the three jars in a basket and called for Adam to come.

Outside, Adam scooted onto the center of the bench, and Cade lifted Emily up. Her insides ached to be seated next to her husband. The past few days, he'd touched her often, though he had yet to kiss her again. But he had said he'd wanted to take it slowly. Was she brazen for wanting him to go faster?

As they bumped along the dusty road, with Adam's little body tossing against hers, she realized God had given her everything she'd wanted. Adam was a child of her own heart, and as much as she wanted Cade's love, it wasn't because of what he could give her. A warm, soft feeling tickled her insides. She loved Adam so dearly. He was her son in every way that counted. She reached over then and pulled him close to her. He looked up, those big blue eyes so trusting and vulnerable, and smiled sweetly. She laid a kiss on his hair.

When they arrived in town, Cade helped them down from the wagon, then he ran over to the feed store, promising to meet them shortly. Emily carried her basket of preserves into the store with Adam trailing closely behind.

The door jangled their entrance, then Emily approached the table where Mrs. Parnell was tidying up a bolt of cloth.

"Well, good day, Mrs. Manning," she said.

"How do, Mrs. Parnell." Suddenly she wondered if the woman had really meant what she'd said about selling her preserves. Perhaps she was only being friendly. She wished she could hide the basket behind her, but its bulk prevented that.

"Can I help you find something?" she asked.

"I—well, I brought these preserves." She held out the basket. "That is, if you still have need of them."

Mrs. Parnell put her age-spotted fingers to her face. "Oh, that's wonderful. Let's see what you brought."

She set the jars on the counter, marveling over the pretty cloth and ribbons. "These'll fetch a fine price. I'd love to try your strawberry and boysenberry as well, if they're up to the same standards as your marionberry."

"They're yummy!" Adam said from her side. "Sometimes I want to skip the biscuits and eat the preserves right from the spoon!"

Mrs. Parnell laughed.

"Adam!" Emily scolded.

"Well, it's probably true, Dear, your marionberry is mighty fine indeed."

They settled on a price, and Emily left the store, eager at the thought of making money of her own. They shopped a bit, then went out to where Cade waited for them. After he assisted them up, they started off.

As they passed the post office, the postmistress came running out the door. "Mrs. Manning!" she called.

Cade slowed the horses to a stop while the postmistress ran into the road. "You've a letter, Dear." She handed up a well-handled envelope.

"Thank you," Emily said.

As she looked at the heavy scrawling on the envelope, she could feel Cade looking over her shoulder. "From your uncle?" he asked.

She nodded, anxiety worming through her and drying her throat.

As Cade gave the reins a yank, she tucked the letter into the pocket of her skirt. Part of her wanted to rip the package right open, but the smarter part of her knew she'd better wait until she was alone. There was no telling what Uncle Stewart had to say, but she was certain it was nothing that would benefit her fragile relationship with her husband.

thirteen

Once Cade set off to the back pasture and Adam got settled with his marbles, Emily sat at the desk and ripped open the envelope. Her uncle's handwriting was scrawled hastily across the paper, and she read quickly.

> *Emily,*
>   *I'm advising you that I have put your grandmother in the asylum.*

Emily sucked in a breath, her heart beating against her ribs in fear. *Oh, no!*

> *As you know, her health has continued to decline so I am no longer able to take care of her here. You have expressed interest in taking care of the old woman, but you have failed to fulfill our agreement. Until you find the gold, which I might remind you is the reason you were sent there in the first place, your grand-mother will remain in the institution. As her legal guardian, I will do with her as I see fit since she is not of her own mind.*
>   *If you will bring yourself to continue the search, I will consider handing over guardianship to you. Though, I must admit, I'm growing increasingly irritated by your games.*

The gist of it is this: if you want your precious grandmother out of the institution, you must find the gold and quick. I'll not wait an eternity whilst you whittle away your days.

Uncle Stewart

Emily covered her face with trembling hands. Oh, sweet Nana in the institution! Emily had been there once to visit a friend's mother and had seen the deplorable conditions of the facility. And the treatment of the patients was something to be feared! Some had their hands bound about their waists, and some were strapped to their beds and left moaning with nary a soul to comfort them.

Oh, Nana, have they done this to you as well? She brushed away the tears that had fallen on her cheeks. How selfish of her to become so taken with her life here that she actually thought Uncle Stewart might give up on getting his gold. She'd been thinking only of herself.

She lay her head against the hard surface of the desk and allowed herself a good cry. When she finished, she smoothed the letter and stuffed it back into the envelope. She had to find that gold, that's all there was to it.

Outside the window, Adam picked up a stick and used it as a gun toward the grove of trees. "Pow, pow, pow!"

How could she search the caves when she'd promised Cade she'd not take Adam there again? Besides her promise, she couldn't risk his safety.

Her heart grew heavy at the thought of deceiving her husband again, just when things were starting to go right. The heaviness turned leaden when she thought of justifying the hours she'd spend away from the house. Would

Cade grow to mistrust her? How could she keep up such deceit? *Lord, I know it's wrong to deceive my husband, but what choice have I?*

Tell him.

But I can't! I can't tell him the truth. That I'd only come to marry his brother because of the gold. He'll never trust me again, and rightly so!

Tell him.

I can't!

There must be some other way. If she could only find that gold, all this would be over with and she and Cade and Adam could go on as if all this never happened. Cade would never have to know, and he would be free to love her, to trust her.

Yes. That was the best thing to do.

But how to search the caves when she had to protect Adam. That was the problem. If she could just solve that, her dilemma would be over. If she could just figure some way to keep Adam safe while she searched the caves.

Mara.

≈

It was late afternoon by the time Emily made it over to Mara's house. She found her friend bent over an onion plant, knees planted firmly in the rich soil. Down the row, Beth stood and stretched, her skirts billowing in the breeze.

Adam ran ahead. "Beth!"

The girl walked toward them, and Mara stood, stretching her shoulders back with her hands on her hips. Her bonnet flapped in a mock wave, and Emily saw the smile that bloomed on her face.

"Emily, Adam, to what do we owe this pleasure?"

"I wanna show Beth my new aggie!" Adam said. The two youngsters ran to a spot under a shade tree and started a game of marbles.

Fear sucked the moisture from Emily's mouth as she thought of what she must tell her new friend. The relationship was too new to be tested in this way. What if Mara wanted nothing to do with her or her rotten scheme? What if Mara told Cade what she'd been up to all this time? Her insides quaked with the weight of it.

As the women approached each other under the hot summer sun, the smile slipped from Mara's face. "What's wrong?" Mara took her arm.

Emily tried for a smile. "Everything's fine. I just. . .I just have some things to tell you. I need your help." She said the last with all the desperation she felt.

Mara squeezed her hand. "You know I'll do anything I can. Come inside; let's have a glass of lemonade."

As they entered the house, Emily's stomach churned with doubt. Maybe there was some other way. Sure, Mara was willing to help a friend, but that was before she knew that Emily had married Cade under false pretenses. Before she knew that she'd been deceiving her husband all these weeks. What would she think of Emily when she knew the truth? At the thought of losing her only friend, a heavy weight settled in her middle.

She took a seat on the sofa while she waited for Mara to fetch the lemonade. How would Mara react? There was no way of knowing, especially since she really hadn't known her all that long. But even so, she felt their bond of friendship was strong. And Emily had already gone over all her options. This was the only one she had. The safest one she had. She had to find that gold without Cade knowing about it. If the thought of losing Mara made her sad, the thought of losing Cade just when things were coming along sent prickles of terror through her. No, she must do what she'd come to do.

Mara entered the room and set down the lemonade. Emily took a long sip and complimented Mara on the taste.

"Enough small talk, Emily. What's going on? You look as if you're being chased by a band of renegades."

Emily tested Mara with a glance, then fastened her gaze on the glass in her hands. "I have some things to tell you that will surprise you. I'm afraid what I say will be a bitter disappointment to you. And I'm afraid you'll think me a horrible person."

"Nonsense." Mara squeezed her arm. "Nothing you can say will make me think that. We all do silly things sometimes. Believe me, I should know about that with all the shenanigans I've pulled."

Emily remembered some of the stories she'd heard about Mara. Stories of things she'd done and said before she became a child of God. Maybe she would understand. With trembling hands and a quaking spirit, she told Mara the truth. All the way from her uncle finding the map to her agreement to marry Thomas in order to have access to the farm. From finding about Thomas's death to accepting Cade's proposal; then her refusal to search for the gold and her uncle's news that he'd put Nana in the asylum.

Throughout the story, Emily carefully avoided Mara's gaze, but when she mentioned that her grandmother was now in an asylum, she heard Mara gasp. It was all the encouragement she needed to meet her friend's gaze.

Mara's sky-blue eyes were widened, her delicate skin drawn. "That's awful," she whispered.

"I know what I've done is wrong, but I only did it for Nana's sake, don't you see?"

Mara's gaze found her lap. "I understand why you did it, truly." She met Emily's gaze. "It was wrong, mind you, what you did to Cade, using him that way."

"I know. I know." Guilt bore into her stomach, filling it with a week's worth of shame and embarrassment.

Mara brushed a smudge of dirt from her skirt. "Well, there's only one thing to make this right."

Oh, thank You, Lord, she understands! If I only find the gold, all this deceit will be over and done with. She felt a deep urge to hug her friend.

"You must tell Cade, of course," Mara said.

Emily settled back into the sofa, feeling her the skin on her face sag with disbelief. No. No, she couldn't do that. He'd never forgive her, never trust her, couldn't Mara see that?

"No," Emily said, but the word came out a croak.

"Emily, you have to. You can't go on deceiving him anymore. It's not right. God is displeased with—"

"Don't you think I know that?" The words were too loud, and she immediately regretted them. Especially when Mara shifted uncomfortably.

"I'm sorry," Emily said. "I have no aught against you." She grabbed Mara's arm, desperate for her friend to understand. "Cade is finally starting to care for me. After all these weeks, he's tender with me, and he's treating me like his wife." She looked down. "Well, almost." The heat she felt in her face left no doubt Mara understood.

"Still, Emily, it's lying." Mara shook her head and looked away. "You have no idea who you're talking to. I'm the queen of lies. Or at least, I used to be."

"I've heard stories," Emily admitted, berating herself for listening to the gossip.

"They're all true, I'm sure, every last one. I shamed myself time and time again, and believe you me, I made no friends in doing so."

"But you got Clay."

She gave a brittle laugh. "That was God's work, rest assured. I began our relationship under pretense, just as you have done with Cade." Her face filled with color. "He needed a housekeeper and caretaker for Beth, and I pretended I was up to the task."

"How is that pretense?" Emily knew Mara to be a fine homemaker and mother to Beth.

"Oh, Emily, you've no idea how I've changed since then. I was raised in the lap of luxury with nary a thought for anyone other than my own self. I'd never cooked or cleaned, and certainly never fed hogs."

A smile sneaked up on Emily's face as she tried to imagine Mara doing those things for the first time.

"It was a disaster, I assure you. Oh, I was able to hold it together for awhile, but eventually things came crashing down around me. Clay found out the truth, and I was caught."

"This is different, though. I'm doing this for Nana. I can't allow my uncle to leave her in the asylum!"

Mara squeezed her hand. "Of course you can't. But as hard as it will be, you must be honest with Cade."

"No. I won't do it, Mara." Didn't her friend understand how delicate Cade's feelings for her were? If he found out how she'd tricked him all this time, it would ruin things for sure. Her eyes stung with tears. "Yes, I married Cade for all the wrong reasons. But I've come to love him. And finally, after all these weeks, he's beginning to care for me too." Emily stood and walked to the window, letting the sunlight warm her skin.

There was only silence behind her, and she wondered if Mara was beginning to come around. The thought sent hope bubbling to the surface. She turned.

"I know it's not right, but I just need to get this over with. I need to find the gold and give it to my uncle, then I can get my grandmother back, and Cade won't have to know about any of it."

"All this aside, the stolen loot belongs to the bank, Emily. Giving it over to your uncle is stealing."

Emily blinked. "What else am I to do, Mara?"

"Why did you come to me, Emily?" Mara asked quietly.

In her rush to tell the story, she'd forgotten to tell Mara about Adam. "Awhile back, Adam and I got lost in a cave, and Cade became very worried. He forbade me from taking Adam into the caves anymore." She walked to her friend and knelt at her feet.

"But that's where the gold is buried. I can't take Adam to the caves anymore, and I thought perhaps. . ."

Mara tucked in the corner of her lip. "You want me to look after Adam while you search."

"Yes." She took her friend's hand and let the desperation she felt in her soul shine in her eyes. "Please, Mara. Just in the afternoons. I'll be back before you get supper on, and he won't be any problem, I promise."

"I know he won't be any trouble; Adam's a fine boy." Mara looked away, and Emily knew she was weighing her options.

"It won't take me long to find the gold, if I can just focus on that. Then all this will be over. Nana will come here, and

Cade. . .Lord willing, Cade will find himself falling in love with me too." The tears that blurred her vision slipped quietly down her face. Her insides froze with Mara's indecision, and, at the same time, she felt gooseflesh tighten her skin.

Mara sighed deeply. "All right, I'll do it."

Emily embraced her friend, gratitude welling in her.

"I'll do it, Emily, but I still think what you're doing is wrong."

Emily squeezed Mara's shoulders. "You won't regret it, I promise."

fourteen

Cade watched Emily scrubbing the dishes through the open kitchen door. Her fine shoulders tapered down to the narrowest of waists, and, for just a moment, he wondered how her waistline would look thickened with the pregnancy of their child. Heat rose up in his gut and coiled around, loosening a pleasurable sensation. His heart thudded against his ribs at the thought. Emily with child. With *his* child.

Just as quickly, his gut clenched tightly, almost painfully. He remembered the way Ingrid had died after birthing Adam, and fear rose up in him like a whirlwind.

He rubbed his face with roughened hands. Emily was not with child, he reminded himself. He would face those fears when the time came, and he knew—trusted—that time would come.

Though she'd behaved mighty strange this evening, he knew things would work out between them. It was painful, putting the past behind him. Putting Ingrid behind him. But in truth, her face had dimmed more each day, replaced by Emily's vivid features. And each day, he looked forward to coming home to Emily, looked forward to her smiles and tender glances.

Yes, his heart had opened to her, despite his reluctance, and he found his gaze swinging toward her more and more. Even now, his hands itched to touch her. He stood up, draining the last of his coffee and took it into the confines of the kitchen. In the sitting room, he could hear Adam playing with the toy soldiers he'd given him on his last birthday.

When he approached Emily, he reached around her, setting the cup in the water.

She jumped, clearly not hearing his approach over the sloshing water.

"Oh!" She gave a stiff laugh. "I—I didn't hear you."

Maybe he should back away, but the way her face softened, the way her lips curled up so sweetly made his body move closer as if it had a will of its own.

His hands found her shoulders and slid slowly down to her waist. As his hands came around her, the longing for her welled up in him so strongly, his breath caught in his lungs. His hands lay against her abdomen, and despite the fear he'd felt moments earlier, he knew a fierce desire to see Emily carrying their child.

When she lay her head back against his chest, he nearly groaned. Oh, how he wanted this woman as his true wife. How he wanted them to be a real family—he, Adam, and Emily.

He nestled his face in the curve of her neck and felt her shiver. There was nothing in their way now. He was ready to let go of the past and give their relationship a real effort. It was what God intended, he was sure, and what he himself had come to desire above all else.

He turned her in his arms, and when her hands clung to his biceps, he hardly noticed the dishwater that seeped through his shirtsleeves.

He lowered his head toward her and tasted her lips. His heart filled with something sweet and hot, and when she moved her lips tentatively against his, he felt a joy well up in him that belied all reality. He wanted to lose himself in her, had already done so—

A twitter of laughter pulled him reluctantly from a world that contained only the two of them. He turned toward the sound.

"Yer kissing Mama." Adam giggled again. "Beth said kissing's ucky, and her ma and pa do it all the time."

This time the giggle came from Emily.

"Well, that's her opinion," Cade said. "And besides, you're not to be sneaking up on folks like that."

"Why do grown-ups like to kiss so much, Pa?" His wide blue eyes stared back at Cade as guileless as a dove.

"Why do—well, they just do, is all." By the heat coursing under his skin, he felt sure Emily must see a rising tide of red on his face.

"Beth said grown-ups kiss a long time, like you's just doin' with Ma. But when Ma kisses me, it's just a little one. Why's that, Pa?"

He shifted away from Emily and rubbed his neck. "I think you've been talking to Beth too much is what I think. Go get your nightshirt on, it's your bedtime."

"Aww."

"Get on with you now."

"Yes sir." Adam slumped away, his toy soldiers in hand.

Cade dared a glance at Emily. Her eyes brimmed with mirth, and her still-damp hand covered her mouth.

"You think that's funny, do you?"

"Mhmm." She giggled again, and the sound of it tweaked his funny bone. He reached out and poked her in the ribs where he knew she was ticklish.

She jerked away.

"Well, if you're gonna be laughing anyway, I say, let's give the lady a real reason." He dodged toward her again, hands outreached.

She bolted around him and out the kitchen door, squealing like a little girl. He scrambled after her, joy lighting his insides, mindless of the chair he overturned in the process.

❧

Emily nudged the horse, and he jolted into action. In front of her, Adam squeezed his marbles tight in his little fists. He was eager to go play with Beth, but Emily was dreading going back to the caves.

After last night's embrace and the tickle fight that had led to another embrace, the very last thing she wanted to do was go behind her husband's back again. He was falling in love with her, and the thought brought a warm, stirring sensation in her middle that was goodness itself. She already loved him more than life. She looked at the boy at her side and felt her insides turn to mush. Her son. She so loved the way he nudged the hair from his eyes with the jerk of his head. The way his blue eyes turned dark and stormy when he didn't get his way. Yes, he was her son in every way that counted. And, Lord willing, Cade would soon be her husband in every way that counted.

If she could just get this gold found. She nudged the horse again, making him pick up the pace. Last night she'd had an awful dream about Nana. She had been strapped down to her bed whilst all the doctors and nurses stood laughing around her. Emily's heart beat heavily in her chest. It wasn't true, she knew that. But what was going on at that place so far away? Was Nana crying her name in the night as she had in her dream?

Lord, help me find that gold and fast! I can't bear for Nana to be there any longer.

After she left Adam with Mara, she rode back toward the area the map indicated. It seemed futile to search in the cave she'd been in before. Hadn't she dug up practically every scrap of dirt in there?

She rode past the cave's entrance for awhile and around a grove of trees where an open meadow ended into a cliff wall. She looked down at her map, and her heart surged. Was this oblong circle on the paper the meadow? If so, the cave where the gold was buried would be in that cliff wall across the way. She wished the markings were clearer, but the water damage had smeared so much of the map.

Her breaths came in gasps as she trotted the horse across the open field. *Please, Lord, let this be it!*

Reaching the other side seemed to take forever, but when she did, she rode along the face of the cliff looking for an opening. The wall was jagged and tall, jutting out this way and that and covered with weeds and bushes. Tumbleweed had blown up against the face of the cliff and lay trapped against the rocky surface. The cliff went on for quite a distance, varying in height, but her heart sunk as it began to grow shorter and shorter until it was barely over her head.

Then she saw it. Behind a scrubby bush, no higher than a dog's back, and nestled in the rock wall was a little black hole.

fifteen

Emily stabbed the shovel into the dirt once more and pulled up a small pile of ancient earth. She wished the map had been more specific as to the whereabouts of the buried loot, but she was certain she was at least in the right cave. A whole week had passed without finding the gold, but Emily was certain she would find it soon. This cave was much smaller than the one she'd searched before. Only one open chamber and two short tunnels.

She hated that her relationship with Mara was strained each day when she dropped off Adam, but she rested assured that when everything worked out, Mara would see Emily had done the right thing.

She stopped her digging, noting that it must be growing late. She walked the short distance outside the cave to check the sun's position. She should leave now if she wanted to get home in time to get supper on.

She stooped down to enter the cave, wishing the ceilings were a bit higher so she could straighten fully in the main room. She would finish this hole before she left. Just a few more shovelsful, then she would get Adam.

She struck the earth with the shovel once, twice, then three times. She should go a few inches deeper, just to be certain. She hurried, not wanting to take the chance that Cade would return home before she did.

On the last thrust of her shovel, she heard a solid thump.

She stopped a moment, wondering if her ears were playing tricks on her in the echoing confines of the cave. She struck the dirt again. *Thump.* A rock? No, she knew very well by now the way the shovel clanked, not thumped against rock.

Her heart accelerated. *Oh please, Lord, let it be!* She removed more dirt and held the lantern above the hole. Something was buried under there. Hopefully not a big log. She ran her fingers ran along the surface and felt chills snake up her spine. This was no log. It was smooth to the touch, with straight grooves across the surface. *A chest.*

She sat back on her haunches, her hands trembling, her insides churning. It was late; she had to get Adam and go home. She straightened as much as she could under the damp ceiling. It would take too long to dig out the chest tonight. She would have to wait until tomorrow. The thought nearly killed her. She'd waited so long to find it, and now she had to leave it here!

She dusted off her skirts. Well, there was no help for it. Besides, the gold had been here for ages, it certainly wasn't going anywhere.

As she left the cave and rode to collect Adam, she gave praise to the Lord. Soon this would be over, and she and Cade and Adam would be a real family at last. Cade would never have to know the ugliness that had brought her here to begin with.

Later that night, when the house was quiet and she was alone in her room, she pulled her diary from the bottom of a drawer.

> *Dear Diary,*
>   *I have found the gold at last. I am so excited that this*

ruse is almost over. I wish I could give Nana a hug and
assure her she'll be in my care soon, but alas, that is
impossible. It's all I can do to wait until tomorrow.
The gold is buried in a chest, and though I have yet to
unearth it, I could see its rounded top buried a foot or so
under the ground. I'm so thankful to Mara for watching
Adam for me.

Diary, my heart beats rapidly even now as I think
about finishing this job. I can hardly wait for it to be
done so I can focus solely on my husband and child. Oh,
to be a regular farmer's wife! I will be so relieved not to
have this dreadful search hanging over my head.

❧

Emily took the eggs she'd collected from her basket and, one
by one, cracked them into the skillet. They sizzled and
smoked, their yolks staring up at her like the bright sun
dawning outside. A course of energy had flowed through her
veins all night and every moment since she she'd awakened.
Chores had been done in record time; she could not wait to
get back to the cave. But wait she must because Mara had
plans this morning and couldn't watch Adam.

She would just have to bide her time until the afternoon;
then she would go to that cave and unearth what she was
sure was the gold. Part of her couldn't believe she'd found it
so quickly. For that she was so thankful to God! Soon, her
uncle would have his gold, she would have Nana, and Cade
would have the wife he thought she was.

A niggle of guilt coursed through her at the thought of
Cade. *Don't be silly. What he doesn't know won't hurt him.* It
would be a disaster for him to find out now. It would ruin
everything.

She flipped the eggs, letting the underside cook just a moment before scooting them onto a platter. She checked on the biscuits and saw they had a few minutes left to cook. The ham was already on the plate and the table set. She'd just—

Cade's arms circled her waist, and she jumped. Turning her head, she saw Cade's clean-shaven jaw only inches from hers. Her heart did a happy jig. "You mustn't sneak up on me like that."

"Can't help myself." The smile in his voice sent shivers up and down her arms.

She tried for an indignant voice. "Oh, and why is that, Mr. Manning?"

His hand flatted on her sides, shooting hot darts straight to her belly, and she sucked in a breath.

"I've got me a beautiful woman in my kitchen; how am I supposed to keep my hands to myself?" If she was about to take offense at his answer, it was forgotten when he planted the gentlest of kisses on her temple. Immediately, heat flared in the spot his lips touched.

Somewhere in the house, she could hear Adam singing, but her eyes were only for her husband at the moment. The green in them had come out to play, as his boyish lashes drooped lazily over them.

He turned her in his arms, and she could feel his thighs pressed up against hers. Fire kindled in her belly and spread rapidly through her limbs.

He tipped her chin up.

"You are some woman."

The words brought more pleasure to her heart than she'd felt in a long time. She feasted on them like a starving animal and was hungry for more.

His thumb moved tenderly across her chin, and she wondered if he knew he was causing a riot inside her. Oh, how she loved this man. How she longed to be loved by him.

"I have some things I want to tell you, Emmie," he whispered. His breath fanned the curls loosened beside her face, and the movement sent shivers across her scalp.

She wondered what it was he wanted to say. She wished she could just drag the words from his mouth, but she had to be patient.

She was vaguely aware of tromping on the stairs and knew Adam would be coming down for breakfast. Cade must've heard it too, for she felt him withdrawing.

His hands moved down to her arms. "Plenty of time for this later, I reckon."

Disappointment turned the fire in her belly cold, and her legs felt as wispy as smoke.

Behind her, she heard Adam scooting his chair out from the table. She smothered a sigh.

"But tonight," her handsome husband said, "when Adam's in bed, and I've got you all to myself, I got some things I need to tell you." His eyes promised so much. Love and— dare she hope—the fulfillment of their marriage vows. She was suddenly so grateful she'd made the decision not to tell Cade about the gold.

She nodded, mesmerized by the intense look on his face. "I'll be here."

When he left the kitchen, she started getting breakfast on the table, and despite the delay of Cade's words, she knew she had reason for that extra spring in her step.

She almost croaked when Adam asked if they were going over to Beth's again today. When she said yes, Cade had looked at her and said, "Sure are spending lots of time over at the Stedmans'."

She buttered her biscuits to busy her hands. "We've become fast friends," she said, hoping he wouldn't disapprove. "But I always finish my chores first."

She waited while he finished a bite of eggs. "I think it's good you've become friends."

She breathed a silent sigh of relief and quickly changed the subject to the coming harvest.

The day dragged by so slowly, Emily thought she'd go mad with the waiting. She kept herself busy with her chores, especially the garden. She picked the ripe tomatoes, mopped the floors, wiped down the doors, and made two loaves of bread.

At last, it was time to take Adam to Mara's. She trotted the horse through the meadow, taking the shorter route. The shovel thumped against the horse's side, and Adam bounced in front of her.

When at last they reached the Stedman ranch, Emily whisked Adam down from the horse and hurried to the door. She knocked, her limbs trembling with anticipation. When several moments went by, she knocked again. Maybe Mara was around back tending the garden. She was just about to check when the door squeaked open.

"There you are," Emily said. "I was just about—Mara, what's wrong?" Her friend's face was flushed, her nose an uncomely shade of red, and her eyes look glazed.

Mara put a hand to her head.

"You're sick." The realization left her both sympathetic for her friend and worried that she wouldn't be able to watch Adam. But then, there was always Beth. Perhaps. . ."

"I'm so sorry," Mara said. "I'm not up to watching Adam today."

"Of course you're not. You need to be in bed." She wanted to ask about Beth, but felt ashamed to be so selfish. Still, she could have that gold in her hands today!

"I'd have Beth watch him, but she's at the McClains' today helping Sara. I'm sorry, Emily."

She fought the flood of disappointment that flowed through her. "Don't be silly. Get yourself to bed. Can I make some tea for you?"

"No, no, thanks. I'm sure it's nothing serious, but you don't need to be catching it."

She gave a wan smile. "I'll check on you tomorrow, then. Take care of yourself and get plenty of rest."

Mara nodded and shut the door, and Emily and Adam returned to the horse. Adam whined about not getting to stay until Emily felt impatient with him. What was she going to do? She needed only one more day to unearth the gold, and it would be over. And the timing couldn't be better. Tonight her husband was going to tell her he loved her, she was sure of it. How wonderful it would be to have this mess cleared up beforehand. And there was Nana too. She didn't want her staying in that asylum one day more than she had to. She had to unearth that chest today.

She helped Adam mount the horse, then mounted behind him. Was there anyone else who could watch Adam today? Her mind sifted through the town residents, and she tried to imagine herself asking each of them for the favor. Slowly she eliminated everyone she knew. What reason could she possibly give?

Perhaps. . .

No, you promised you wouldn't.

Still the thought formed fully in her mind. Maybe she could take Adam just this once. After all, the chest was buried only feet from the cave entrance. He could play outside, by the mouth of the cave where she could hear him. Why, he wouldn't even have to set foot inside.

She nudged the horse, a tentative smile forming on her face. "Adam, how would you like to go on an adventure today?"

sixteen

Emily scooped another shovelful of dirt and tossed it in the growing pile. Even in the shade of the cave, her skin dripped with sweat. She stopped, letting herself rest against the shovel's handle, and caught her breath. Excitement raced through her veins until she trembled with it. She could see the chest now and had dug until the rounded top was exposed.

The trunk appeared to be wooden and about three feet long, smaller than she had imagined. The color was a rich brown, though since it was dirt-stained, there was no telling its original color.

She picked up the shovel and began digging again. Outside, she could hear Adam talking to himself as he played in the grass under a tall tree with his soldiers. She couldn't believe how perfectly everything was working out. Even with Mara sick, with the digging site so close to the cave entrance, it was easy enough to listen for him.

She dug deeply on the side of the chest and saw the dark metal loops attached to the side. Her heart thumped heavily in her chest, both from exertion and anticipation.

"Whatcha doing?" Adam's voice came from inside the doorway of the cave.

"Adam, you're not to be in here."

"Why does that tree have arms?"

"What? What are you talking about?"

He pointed out toward the spot he'd been playing in. "It

goes like this." He forked his hands showing her how the tree was one trunk that split into two.

She had to get him out of here. "It's called a schoolmarm tree, Honey. It just grows that way. Now, you need to go back outside."

"Did you find treasure?" he asked.

For a moment a dash of anxiety prickled her skin, then she remembered all the times she'd buried his marbles and knew the child couldn't know the truth.

She stepped around the hole, not wanting him to see there really was something under the dirt. Something very big and valuable. She mustn't let him see it or he would say something to his pa for sure. She wondered idly how she would get the chest out of the cave and to her uncle.

"Let's go back outside," she said, ushering the boy through the little opening. "I shouldn't be much longer, then we'll go home and have supper."

"Can we have corn cake?"

"We'll see." Emily slipped through the doorway and resumed her digging. She would have to leave the chest here and come back for it when Adam wasn't with her. And how would she get it to her uncle? How did one go about shipping a chest full of stolen gold coins? Perhaps she should wire her uncle and have him come get it. Yes, that would be the safe thing to do. But first, she would insist he take Nana out of the asylum. He could bring her with him when he came for the gold. She wouldn't give him his precious loot until he brought Nana safe and sound.

She moved to the front of the chest and began digging. Her mind wandered back to this morning when Cade had embraced her. Shivers ran up her arms even as heat curled in her belly. What had he been about to say when Adam had come downstairs? It was torture having to wait an entire day to hear his words, but the promise in his eyes left little doubt that he'd fallen in love with her.

Her heart skittered faster, and a smile tilted her lips. Would tonight be their first night together as man and wife? She could hardly believe it was happening, and yet she'd seen the love shining in Cade's eyes. Why, she might yet get to experience the feeling of a child growing within her. Cade's child.

Her stomach clenched at the thought. A baby brother or sister for Adam would be just the thing.

"I'm bored." Adam's whine from the cave's entrance scared her.

"Adam. You're supposed to be playing outside."

"I wanna come in here with you."

When he approached, she stepped in front of the hole. She had to keep him occupied safely, outside the cavern, if she ever wanted to get this gold dug up. "Would you like me to bury some marbles for you?"

"In here?" He dug the marbles from his pocket.

"No, Adam, your pa said—"

Adam threw down his marbles and stomped a dirty boot. "I wanna stay in here with you, Ma." His tears welled up; she could see them even in the dim light of the cave. "Please. . ."

Emily sighed and looked over her shoulder at the chest, still half covered with dirt. Well, she knew there were no wild animals in the cave, and that had been Cade's biggest concern. Besides, it wouldn't take long at all to finish.

"All right. But just this once."

Adam clapped his hands and bounced on his feet.

"But you have to stay over there near the entrance." She

wanted to add that he couldn't tell his pa but couldn't bring herself to do it. Lying herself was bad enough; she wouldn't teach Adam to do it too.

She walked over with her shovel and began digging. "Turn around, so you can't peek."

When he did as she said, she continued digging until she had each marble hidden, then she covered the spot with the fresh dirt. "There you go. Stay over here, understand?"

"Yes Ma'am!" Adam was already on his hands and knees pawing through the dirt.

She walked back to her hole, keeping the lantern closer to Adam so he couldn't see the chest. She worked hard, removing the packed earth from around the wooden exterior. Every few minutes, Adam would let out a squeal when he found another marble.

Soon, she had all but one corner of the chest unearthed. There seemed to be a rock or something equally hard against this side of the chest, for she made very slow progress. Finally, she began stabbing harder and harder at the dirt with her shovel blade. Sweat beaded on her forehead, and her back strained with every downward slice. She grunted under the effort, her arms aching.

Then she heard something. Something that started quietly, like the rumble of a stampede off in the distance. But it grew louder. She stopped and listened, holding her shovel still.

Gravel slid down the wall beside her as the rumble grew louder, and all of a sudden it dawned on her. The cave was going to collapse.

She threw down her shovel just as larger rocks began to fall around them. The rumble was so loud she had to shout as she ran toward Adam. "Get out!"

Adam stood, his eyes wide with fright, and his feet rooted to the ground. As if in slow motion, she saw a rock break loose from the wall above him.

"Moooove!" She reached out and shoved him out of the way, toward the entrance. Her feet found the hole he was digging, and she stumbled, falling just feet from the cave's entry.

"Ma!"

Her head smacked the hard floor of the cave, and the rock that had fallen hit her calf with the force of a cannonball. She cried out, barely recognizing her own voice. The rock's rough edges tore into her skin, the weight of it crushed her bones.

seventeen

"Ma!" Adam knelt beside her.

"Get out," she rasped. "Hurry!" The rumble had turned to a loud roar.

"You're hurt!"

He tried to tug on the rock, but she knew it was too heavy for him. "Get out, Adam!" What if a rock fell on him too? She couldn't bear the thought of her boy being hurt or worse. It was only then she realized the roaring she heard was in her head, and that the rumbling had stopped. No more rocks fell, only bits of gravel. Fear still rattled between her ears and pumped through her veins.

She wet her lips, her cheek smashed into the dirt. "Adam, listen to me."

The boy kept trying to dislodge the rock, and each time it moved a tiny fraction, she moaned in agony. "Adam, stop!" He sat back on his haunches, then crawled up where he could see her face.

"It's stuck, I can't move it." Tears streaked through the dirt on his face, and his little lips quivered.

She reached out and took his hand. The pain got the best of her, and her teeth began chattering. It was taking all her effort not to cry out. "Listen, Adam. I need your help. You have to go home. Get your pa and show him where I am, can you do that?"

He shook his head. "I don't know how."

"I'll tell you how," she said, stopping for some quick breaths. "But you must listen carefully."

❧

Cade sat on the front porch chair, his elbows propped on his knees. Where were they? He'd been home for a long time, and the sun was finding its home on the horizon already.

He told himself she'd lost track of time. He told himself she was only running late. But a thought kept snagging him like a burr on fleece. A thought he tried to avoid until now. He recalled the words he'd spoken to Emily this morning. He'd made it clear he had something to say to her tonight. Something important.

He was going to tell her he loved her. That he wanted them to be a real family; that he wanted her to be his real wife. All day long he'd thought of little else. But the thought that had lingered in the back of his mind since he'd come home to an empty house, the thought that he'd shoved away each time, surfaced with the stubbornness of a mule.

Maybe Emily didn't want to hear what he had to say. Maybe he'd scared her off with his promise of something important to say.

No, he wouldn't think it, wouldn't let the words form in his mind. Not yet. The sun still had a sliver poking up over the land. It wasn't dark yet. There were a dozen reasons she might be late.

Cade watched the sun melt silently into the prairie grass. He watched the darkness fall over the ground like a smothering shroud; heard the crickets and cicadas start their oscillating songs.

Maybe she really didn't have feelings for. . .

She probably went over to the Stedmans' again today and—

Mara. If Emily weren't over there, her friend might know where she was.

He ran to the barn and saddled up Sutter, noticing for the first time that Bitsy wasn't in her stall. Now, worry clawed at his insides. This was just like last time when she'd taken Adam to a cave and gotten lost. At least he could scratch that worry from his list. She wouldn't go against his decision to keep Adam away from the caves.

He swung himself up on Sutter and took off across the field toward the Stedmans'. His heart threatened to burst from his chest as he rode. He was starting to think either she or Adam had hurt themselves. She knew better than to be riding at night.

When he arrived at the Stedmans', they were just finishing supper.

"Cade, what brings you out tonight?" Clay asked.

"Can I get you some coffee?" Mara asked. Her cheeks were too pink, and her eyes drooped tiredly.

Cade stepped through the door and shook his head no. "Have you seen Emily today, Mara?"

She looked down at the floor before meeting his gaze again. "What's wrong, Cade?"

"She isn't home. Wasn't there when I got home and still isn't. Adam's with her. Have you seen her?"

She looked at her husband before answering. "She was by this afternoon. Around three o'clock."

"Did she say where she was going?" Cade asked.

Her jaw went slack, and Cade thought her face grew even more red. When she wavered on her feet, her husband led her to the sofa. "She's been sick today," he explained to Cade. "I told her she shouldn't be up fixing supper. You all right, Angel?" he asked his wife.

"I'm fine." Mara settled back against the sofa and closed her eyes, rubbing her face like a tired toddler. Beth must've been washing the supper dishes, for he could hear the clanking in the kitchen.

"Sorry to bother you like this, but I'm worried about Emily and Adam."

"Of course you are. I–I think I might know where they went," Mara said. "I think they went to a cave out toward the cotton tree grove."

Cade shook his head. "I told her not to take Adam to the caves; she wouldn't do that."

Mara studied her hands as they picked at the ribbon on her dress. There was only one word for the expression on her face. Guilt. Could Emily have gone against his decision? No, she wouldn't risk Adam's safety any more than he would.

"I was supposed to watch Adam this afternoon, but with me being sick. . .I think she went ahead anyway."

Cade's thoughts seemed to be flowing as slow as molasses. He couldn't make sense of what Mara was saying. The Emily he knew wouldn't go against him that way for no good reason.

He shook his head again. "She must've gone someplace else. Emily wouldn't defy me like that."

"Mara?" her husband asked. His gaze trained on his wife's face, he seemed to see something Cade was missing. "What's going on?"

Mara wet her lips, meeting her husband's gaze, then Cade's. "I promised I wouldn't tell."

At her words, hope stirred in his heart, but at the same time dread twisted his gut. "They might be in danger, Mara. I need you to tell me anything you know."

Mara bit her lip, then met his gaze. "She's been looking in the caves for some stolen loot that was buried there years ago by your grandfather and hers. She didn't want to take Adam—she hasn't since you told her not to," she said in defense of her friend.

"Stolen loot?" Cade wondered if Mara's fever had gone to her head. Even her husband was looking at her funny. But it was getting late, and Emily and Adam might be hurt.

She sighed, clearly reluctant to go any further. "I guess I better start at the beginning."

Cade cut her off. "I want to hear all about this, but not right now. If you're right about the cave, there's no time to lose."

Clay stood up. "I'll go with you. You be all right, Mara?"

She nodded.

"Thanks," Cade said to Mara.

"I'm sure they're fine," Mara said.

Emily and Adam would be home if they were fine.

❦

The two men rode their horses out across the Stedman property toward the cotton tree grove. There was a cave on a small cliff over there. He'd never been in it, but he feared it was the one Emily had gotten lost in before. Maybe her lantern had burnt out, and they were just lost, like before.

When they reached the cave, they dismounted the horses and untied the lanterns. He couldn't see or hear anything suggesting Bitsy was tied up nearby, but he had to search the cave anyway.

"We'll need something to mark our way; this is a deep cave with lots of tunnels," Cade said.

"I think I have some corn kernels in my pocket," He checked and nodded. "We can drop them as we go."

They split up inside the cave, each with a handful of kernels and a lantern. Cade called out for Emily and Adam, but all Cade heard was his own echo and Clay's calls. He got almost dizzy with all the turns and twists in the tunnel. In places he had to crawl. He could see footprints in the dirt, but he knew they could be weeks old. When he finally worked his way back to the entrance, Clay waited there.

"They can't be in there," his friend said.

Cade shook his head, knowing he was right.

"Where else?"

"There are plenty of caves." He tried to ignore the hopeless tone in his voice. "Hard to tell which one they might have gone to." It was pitch-black out now, and he realized he'd been gone for a couple hours. "Maybe they're home now."

"I can go check if you've a mind to keep looking."

He nodded thoughtfully. "I'll be at the cave by the fallen oak back by Wallen Creek," Cade said as he mounted his horse.

"If they're at your house, I'll come for you. And if they're not, I'll come back and help you look." Clay took off on his mare, and Cade set off for Wallen Creek.

As he rode, he called out for his wife and son. If anything had happened to them. . .

A long while later, he exited the cave. It had opened only to one small room, and there was no sign Emily had even been in this one. He waited outside the entrance, his back propped up against the rough, moss-covered stone.

God, please help them to be all right. Take care of Emily and my boy, and please help me find them.

It was torture waiting here for Clay's return. He fought the urge to go and search other caves, but the truth was that, he wasn't sure of their whereabouts. He'd seen other caves in passing, but this land was not as familiar as his farming acreage. How would he find them in the dark with only a lantern to guide his way? *I need Your help, Father.*

He lay his head against the hard stone and closed his eyes. What was that loot Mara had mentioned, and why had Emily been looking for it? Why had she taken Adam along? It just didn't add up, and he wished he'd let Mara finish the story. A lot of good it had done him to rush off. Now here he sat just waiting—

"Pa!" The cry came from a short distance away and accompanied the sound of hoofbeats. His heart thudded in his throat. His son was all right!

He rose to his feet, his legs trembling beneath him. When Clay's horse came into view, he saw his son, safe and sound in the circle of his friend's arm. Adam's face was wet, streaked with dirt and tears, but otherwise he looked all right.

"Adam." He felt the sting of tears in his eyes at the sight.

"You found them." Cade said as the horse drew to a halt in front of him.

Clay shook his head, but his son spoke. "Ma's hurt, Pa. R—real bad." The tears started again as he drew his son off the horse and into his arms. The boy's little arms wrapped around his neck.

"I g—got lost, and it got dark."

"I know, I know, you're all right now. Papa's got you." He met Clay's gaze.

"Best I can tell," his friend said, "they were in a cave, and it started to collapse. He said a rock fell on Emily's leg, and it was too big to move."

His gut clenched hard. "How bad is she hurt?"

Clay shrugged. "She was conscious at least."

His son loosened his hold and leaned back to meet his gaze. "She said to go home and get you, but I g—got lost."

Hope stirred when he realized Adam knew where she was.

"Do you think you can find the cave, Son?"

"I don't know."

At Cade's request, he described the terrain, narrowing down the location to a few areas. His description of the cliff made him think right off of Potter's Ridge.

He looked at Clay. "Let's mount up. I think I might know the area he's talking about."

They rode the short distance to the ridge, Adam safe in his arms, and Cade thanked God for his son's safety. But Emily's injuries. . . *Lord, keep her safe 'til we find her.*

❧

"It's no use," Cade whispered. They'd searched the ridge over and again, and there was no cave there. Adam had said the entrance was small, but even so, they'd searched the walls on foot, even looking behind all the brush.

Clay had stopped, his lantern hanging in his hand, his gaze trained on Cade. Shadows played over his features, and Cade thought how weary his friend looked. Pity shone from the depths of his eyes. "Your boy's tuckered," Clay said.

Cade looked down and saw his son had slumped against a rock and fallen asleep. He sighed. She wasn't here at Potter's Ridge. Worry filled his belly with a burning sensation. He hated thinking of her lying in the dark somewhere suffering.

"We can keep looking if you want to," his friend said.

Cade's gaze swung across the darkened land. The trees were black against the starlit sky. It would be like looking for a needle in a haystack to continue searching tonight. Maybe Mara had information that would help them locate the cave. Or maybe Adam would be able to find his way back to it in daylight.

"No," Cade said. "It's useless." He hated even saying it. Felt like he was betraying his wife to leave her out there all night. *Dear Lord, protect her tonight. Be there for her in a way I can't.*

"Why don't I take the boy back to our house?" Clay said. "You can come by at dawn and we'll head out again."

Cade shook his head. "I'd like to talk with your wife tonight, if it's all right. She might know something helpful." If she did, he could come back out by himself.

They mounted up and headed back for the Stedman ranch. Adam slept all the way and barely stirred when Cade swung him off Sutter and carried him up to a spare bed.

Mara had waited up, and her face broke out in a smile of relief when she saw Adam in his arms. But tears gathered in her eyes when Clay told her they hadn't found Emily.

After putting his son to bed, Cade sat in a chair across from Mara and her husband. "It was just too dark," Cade said to Mara. "I was hoping you might know something. . .anything that might help us find Emily tonight."

Mara put a trembling hand to her lips and shook her head. "I just know she was west of your house. She never said exactly where she was looking. What did Adam say? Is she hurt bad?"

Cade filled her in as best he could, and together the group prayed for Emily's safe return. It filled him with regret to think he might have lost the chance to tell Emily he loved her. Sorrow welled up in him like a big, black storm.

The prayer ended, and suddenly he remembered what Mara had said earlier about the stolen loot and something about his grandfather.

"I don't understand what you were saying earlier," he said to Mara. "What's this loot Emily was looking for, and how was my grandfather involved?"

Mara closed her eyes briefly. He was asking her to betray her friend, but he knew she must be weighing out the benefits of finding some clue that might help find her. "Apparently your grandfather and hers robbed a bank years ago. Her uncle found a map that showed your farm as the burial spot. A note on the map indicated there was another map hidden at your house."

"I don't know anything about this." He wanted to deny his grandfather's involvement, but he remembered the man's absence and eventual disappearance. "What's Emily got to do with it?" An ugly feeling was stirring in his gut, and he almost didn't want to hear the answer, knew instinctively he wouldn't like it.

Mara seemed reluctant to answer, and the feeling of foreboding grew until his head swam with it.

"Her uncle forced her to come here," Mara said. "She was supposed to marry Thomas, as you know, but then he died, and you asked her to marry you."

"Forced how?" Cade asked.

"Has she told you about her grandmother back home?"

"A little."

"Well, apparently her uncle is her grandmother's guardian, and she has some problems with her memory and such. I didn't get all the details. But her uncle is no gentleman. At first, he threatened he would put her grandmother in an asylum if she didn't go through with the marriage."

He knew she'd written Thomas a letter originally, and that had started their correspondence. Had she done all that to finagle a marriage proposal? Just so she could get at the map and have access to the caves?

His heart sunk to his boots, and he felt like he'd swallowed a walnut for the ache in his throat. She'd wormed her way into Thomas's heart, tricked him into proposing? She'd wormed her way into *his* heart. Into *his* life. Into his son's life. All for the purpose of digging up some stolen gold?

"It's not what you're thinking, Cade," Mara said. "She did it for her grandmother, whom she loves dearly. She hated having to do it."

Hated being married to him? Hated having to pretend. . .

He rubbed his hands over his face to stop the stinging in his eyes. Had she pretended all along? Pretended to care for him, pretended to enjoy his kisses?

"She cares about you, truly." Fervency shone from Mara's eyes. "I'm not explaining this well." Tears escaped her eyes and coursed down her face. "She had stopped looking for the gold after you told her you didn't want Adam in the caves. She had written her uncle and told him she wouldn't do it anymore. She was starting to. . .care for you. She didn't want to deceive you anymore—"

"Then why didn't she just tell me?" His voice boomed louder than he'd expected.

"She was afraid she'd lose your trust. Can't you see, she valued that so much. Her uncle wrote her back that he'd put her grandmother in the asylum and wouldn't take her out until she found the loot. She felt trapped."

His jaw clenched. "So she started searching again."

Mara nodded, dabbing at the tears on her face.

He could hardly believe this. The lies she must've told, the deceit. Maybe she didn't care for him at all. Him or Adam. Maybe it was all just a giant ruse to get at that loot. The thoughts came quickly, each blacker than the one before it, swirling like a twister.

He got up and walked to the window. His temples throbbed with pain, his jaw clenched tightly. How could this be? When he'd thought he loved her?

"Please, Cade, you have to believe me." Mara had approached and took hold of his arm. "She cares deeply for you. She was so afraid of losing your. . .trust."

"So afraid she's lied to me all these months?" He set his hat back on his head. He looked up the stairs where his son slept. How would this affect his boy? He lay upstairs as innocent as a lamb. He'd been in tears over the thought of losing his ma.

Cade sighed. As hopeless as it seemed, as angry as he was with Emily, he would go back out looking tonight. For Adam's sake.

eighteen

Emily heard a moan and tried to move. Her leg screamed with agony. Her eyes opened. At least she thought they did, but the darkness didn't recede. Her arms tightened with gooseflesh, and she felt damp.

She remembered now. She was in the cave, and she'd sent Adam home to his pa. But how long ago was that? The lamp must have flickered out sometime during the night, using up all the oil in the reservoir. There had been hours of light in the oil. Adam should've been back by now.

Please, dear God, let Adam be all right!

What if he'd never made it home? What if he was wandering alone in the darkness? Her eyes stung with silent tears.

What have I done? Oh, dear Lord, what have I done?

She'd endangered her son's life and her own too. A sharp stab of pain shot up her leg, and she gasped. She cradled her head in her arm, smelling the dirt and mustiness of the cave, tasting it in her mouth. Fear snaked up her spine and branched out to every part of her body. What if Adam never made it home? What if he died because of her? She deserved it herself; it was her own fault for going through with this awful plan. Her fault for deceiving Cade.

He would be worried sick by now and surely was out searching for them both. She struggled to think straight, in spite of the searing pain. Her brain seemed stuffed with fog, and she waited a moment until it passed.

How would Cade know where to find them? Perhaps Adam had found his way home but he couldn't find the cave in the darkness. *Oh, please let it be so!* If only Adam made it safely through, she would be ever so grateful.

What would Cade do if Adam couldn't find the cave? How would he find her? A thought sprung up, bringing with it both hope and despair. Would he go to Mara's? Would she tell him everything about her uncle and the loot?

At first she denied it. Mara was a loyal friend, and she wouldn't betray her confidence.

But Emily's life was at risk, and that changed everything, didn't it?

Her heart raced at the thought of Cade learning everything. She closed her eyes and buried her face in her arm. If he found out everything, it was all over. He wouldn't trust her. Wouldn't love her. How could he when she'd deceived and betrayed him so?

Lord Jesus, I was so wrong! Wrong to deceive my husband and wrong to sin against You. Forgive me, Lord.

She should have refused to do her uncle's bidding or confided in her husband from the beginning. Why was it always so easy to see wrong choices when it was too late to change them?

Another pain shot up her leg, and her head spun with dizziness. She fought the sensation, but the wave overtook her.

≈

Cade drew Sutter to a halt, letting the feelings he'd held back for hours come flowing over him like muddy river water. She'd lied to him about everything. Their marriage was a lie. Their life together was a lie.

Clay's horse drew up beside him, and Cade could feel his friend's gaze on him.

"It's time we call it a night." Hadn't he tried his best to find the woman? It was useless looking in the dark. And even though his heart still longed for her, he knew she'd killed his love for her as surely as he sat here.

"Maybe she'll somehow make it home on her own," Clay offered.

Or maybe she'd never make it home at all. Even though he was angry, even though he knew his feelings had been mocked, he couldn't bear the thought of Emily gone.

"Your boy told me something when I found him tonight. Seeing as how you're so angry right now, I thought you'd best know."

"What is it?"

"You might not like what Emily's done; it's wrong, I'll give you that. But if you're questioning her love for the boy, or for yourself, I'd guess you're wrong about that."

Tired as he was, angry as he was, Cade met his friend's gaze in the lamplight. "What are you talking about?"

"Adam told me what happened when the cave-in started. The boulder landed right where he was standing. . . . Emily pushed him out of harm's way, Cade."

Cade's tongue wouldn't seem to move.

Clay ran his hand through his hair. "Rock that size would've killed the boy. Seems your wife risked her own life for the young 'un."

The news made the anger stirring in his gut slow a fraction. Was it true? Had Emily thrown herself in danger to protect his son? His mind swirled with the thought.

"Don't know if that changes anything, but I thought you should know," his friend said. "You can come by at dawn for me and Adam. We'll be saddled up and ready to go. Let's pray Adam will be able to find the cave in the daylight."

Cade nodded. "Thanks, friend."

By the time Cade reached the house, he was feeling tuckered himself, but his mind worked like a dog that wouldn't let go of a bone. Even after hearing what Emily had done for his son, anger ate at his soul. She'd still deceived him. Maybe she did cotton to his son, maybe she had saved his life, but that didn't change what she'd done.

As he lay in alone in Adam's room, he thought back to all the times he'd touched her, kissed her. She'd set his blood aboil with her tentative responses, but what had been going through that mind of hers? Had she been recoiling in disgust? Had she forced herself to respond?

No. He didn't want to believe it. His gut tightened painfully at the very thought. She'd seemed so genuine. Even Mara was convinced of Emily's loyalty. But with all the lies that had been told, all the secrets, how could he believe anything anymore?

He turned over and punched his pillow hard, trying to settle into a comfortable position. It was only a matter of hours before dawn, and if he wanted to be ready to search, he'd best get some sleep.

But try as he might, even though his body was weary, his active mind wouldn't oblige. He sat up in bed and ran a hand through his hair.

Emily. *Oh, Lord God, I love her.* No matter what she'd done, what she'd said or hadn't said, he loved his wife. And she was out there somewhere, likely suffering in pain while he cozied up in this warm bed. *If only there was some way of finding out where she—*

The map. Mara had said she'd found a map here somewhere. Maybe it was in her room.

He tore off the blanket and ran to his old room, throwing open the door so it bounced against the wall. He scrambled in the darkness to light the lamp, then carried it over to the bedside. The top drawer of her night table turned up her Bible, stationery, and a book.

The second drawer held nothing of help, and he slammed it closed. What if she'd taken the map with her? He ran his hands over his weary eyes. She probably had, of course. He looked around the dimly lit room, watching the shadows flicker in the light. Maybe there was something else.

The letters. Of course, Mara had said she'd been corresponding with her uncle. Perhaps she'd kept them. He tore through her drawers, feeling only a smidgen of guilt at the invasion of privacy. This could be a matter of life and death, and if he could help it, his wife would live, never mind what she'd done.

He scrounged through her clothing, realizing she may have hidden them away. *From you.*

He brushed the thought away. He needed to focus on more important matters right now. His hands searched, the lamp on top of the chest providing him a glimpse of articles of clothing he had no right to see. Suddenly, his fingers closed on something hard. He pulled it up through the filmy clothing. Two bundles of something. Letters. A book.

A rush of excitement buzzed through him, giving him a second wind. One bundle had a letter from Thomas atop the pile. The other stack was from Denver. He sat on the foot of the bed and tore off the ribbon. The letters scattered around him, and he saw they were all from the same man. *It has to be her uncle.* He opened the first one he grabbed.

> *Emily,*
>
> *I'm advising you that I have put your grandmother in the asylum.*
>
> *As you know, her health has continued to decline so I am no longer able to take care of her here. You have expressed interest in taking care of the old woman, but you have failed to fulfill our agreement. Until you find the gold, which I might remind you is the reason you were sent there in the first place, your grandmother will remain in the institution. As her legal guardian I will do with her as I see fit since she is not of her own mind.*
>
> *If you will bring yourself to continue the search, I will consider handing over guardianship to you. Though, I must admit, I'm growing increasingly irritated by your games.*
>
> *The gist of it is this: if you want your precious grand-mother out of the institution, you must find the gold and quick. I'll not wait an eternity whilst you whittle away your days.*
>
> *Uncle Stewart*

Cade set down the letter, an ugly feeling growing in his middle at the words scrawled on the page. What kind of man. . . ?

The date was recent, and it fit with Mara's story. Perhaps Emily had been a helpless pawn in the whole mess.

He read the rest of the letters and felt such frustration well up in him that he realized he wanted to slug this Uncle Stewart. After he read the last letter, he picked up the hardbound book with a plain brown cover. Was it Emily's diary? His heart pounded heavily against his ribs. Did he want to know her innermost thoughts?

Fear sucked the moisture from his mouth. What if her heart was contrary to everything she'd said to him? What if inside she had laughed at his bumbling efforts to court her? Could he stand knowing it, if that were the truth?

He nearly laid the book aside, unwilling to face the possibility, but his friend's words played in his mind.

You might not like what Emily's done; it's wrong, I'll give you that. But if you're questioning her love for the boy, or for yourself, I'd guess you're wrong about that.

Slowly, he opened the book. The first page was dated almost a year ago, and he saw Emily's graceful handwriting slanted across the page. If this were her diary, he needed to see if there was anything that might hint of her location. Any clue what cave she was lying in.

He thumbed through until he came to a more recent date. It was dated the same day as the first letter he'd read.

nineteen

Dear Diary,

My heart is overflowing with so many thoughts and feelings. The first of which is my love for my dear husband. He kissed me tonight, and when he touched me, I thought surely I'd burn up from the inside out. Somehow, when little Adam came around, Cade and I ended up in a tickle chase that reminded me of childhood so long ago. But I have gotten ahead of myself.

Even as these wondrous feelings of love consume me, I am torn apart with guilt and shame. Today I received a letter from Uncle Stewart. He has put Nana in the asylum and threatened to keep her there unless I find the gold. So you see, dear Diary, I am in the most precarious of positions.

While Cade has not professed his love for me, I have sensed it in his touch, in his glorious eyes. I can't for the life of me work up the courage to risk losing his trust. So I must continue that dreadful search tomorrow. My heart fights the thought. I want so much to go forward with our wonderful life here. Cade and Adam have become my precious family, yet Nana needs my help. My heart cries out for the injustice done against her.

It is only because of Mara that I can continue the search without going against Cade's order that Adam stay out of the caves. She has agreed to help me, though she says I should tell Cade the truth.

*Oh, Diary, my heart longs to do exactly that, but I
just can't risk losing his love when I have longed for it
for so long. So tomorrow I will search again, and may
God help me find it quickly for all our sakes.*

Cade let the diary fall to his lap, his eyes stinging with
tears. His heart pummeled his ribs as relief washed over him.
Thank You, Jesus. Even though there was no clue about her
whereabouts, at least her feelings for him, for Adam, were
there in black ink for him to see. He suddenly felt like a
doubting Thomas, needing to see proof in order to believe.

He reread the words of love, feeling warmth flow through
him. She had deceived him, she had made wrong choices, but
she loved him. His wife loved him, and he wanted to jump
onto the rooftop and shout it to the world. She hadn't wanted
to lie and keep secrets from him. She'd felt she had to for her
grandmother's sake. It was just as Mara had said.

He heard a rooster crow and looked toward the window.
The sun would be rising soon, and he would be able to
search for Emily. He thumbed through the pages of the
diary, reading excerpts, hoping for some clue as to where she
was. Her words were balm for his soul, a glimpse of the
woman he'd known all along. A woman who had become
mother to his son, keeper of his heart.

Even though her words brought him comfort, they pro-
vided no information as to her whereabouts. It was all up to
Adam. But would his son remember the way they'd gone?

He stopped right there on the foot of the bed and whispered a prayer for Emily's safety. His gut twisted at the
thought of her lying on the cold cave floor in pain. Was she
even conscious now? What if it were already too late?

He wouldn't allow himself to think like that. Dropping the diary on the bed, he went to gather the supplies he and Clay would need. By the time he saddled up, the first light should be chasing away the darkness.

❧

When he arrived at the Stedmans', Clay and Adam were ready to go. His son gave him a hug and turned wet eyes toward him. "We have to find her, Pa."

Cade patted him on the back. "We will, Son."

Mara waved them off, then Cade spoke to Adam, who was snuggled against his belly. "Can you remember anything? You left here yesterday and went in this direction right?"

"I think so."

Cade sighed and exchanged a glance with Clay. "Do you remember anything at all about the cave?" Cade asked. "Think hard, it's important."

"I wasn't supposed to go inside it. Ma said so. She said to play near the doorway where she could keep her eye on me."

She'd made him play outside where he would be safe. She'd tried to keep her word to him. The thought tightened his gut.

It was then he noticed his Adam sniffling. "It'll be all right; we'll find her." He wrapped his arm tightly around his son.

"If I'd a listened, maybe Ma wouldn't be dying."

The word struck something deep within him. He stopped Sutter and turned Adam in his arms, shaking his shoulders. "Now you listen here. Your ma's not dying. She's not." The ache in his throat cut off his words.

Everything went still around them as Cade watched his son blink back tears, his little chin quivering.

Cade gentled his voice. "We'll find her. Everything's going to be fine, you understand?"

Adam's head bobbed against Cade's chest. He met Clay's gaze and saw his friend blinking hard, his jaw clenched tightly.

They headed in the general direction Mara had told them about, bringing their horses to a gallop. It seemed Adam wouldn't be able to help them find the cave, and he really shouldn't have expected it of a young boy anyway. When they neared the first cave they'd searched the previous night, the mammoth one, Adam perked up.

"I've been here!"

Cade's heart did a heavy flop. "Is this the cave, Adam? Is this where you and Emily came yesterday?"

Adam shook his head. "Not yesterday. We got lost in there."

His hopes shriveled up like a decaying leaf. What if they never found her? What if it were already too late? No, he wouldn't think it.

He looked at Adam who'd perked up, sitting straight up on the horse, looking around with a frown puckered between his brows. Maybe he could jog his son's memory.

"Tell me what the area looked like, where you were yesterday. Outside the cave, where you were playing. . ."

He shrugged. "It was a big grassy field, and there was a cliff. That's where the cave was."

It was nothing more than he'd said the night before. "What were you playing with?"

"My soldiers. The bad guys were behind the tree, and the good guys came and got 'em. *Pow, pow, pow!*"

Beside him, Clay ran a hand through his hair. "Why don't we split up? I can go a ways south—"

"Wait a minute," Cade said. Hadn't Adam said twice now he'd been in a grassy meadow? And then he said there was a tree. It was probably nothing, but. . . "Adam, were there lots of trees? You said it was a field before."

"No, there was just one. It was shaped funny too."

"Shaped funny, how?"

He scrunched up his eyes. "Ma said it was a. . .school tree. . .or some such."

"A school tree?" Clay asked.

Adam shrugged. "Somethin' like that. It was like this." He put his forearms together, letting his hands branch out.

"A schoolmarm tree," Cade said. *A schoolmarm tree. In a meadow, by a cliff.* His heart pounded like a fist inside his chest. "I know where she is."

They rode hard all the way there. Cade's heart felt as if it were thumping as fast and hard as the horses' hooves. It had to be the right place. He'd noticed the tree several times before because it didn't split into two trunks until a good ways up, and he'd always thought it looked like a giant slingshot.

He'd never noticed a cave there in the cliff, but if the entrance was as small as Adam was saying, it was no wonder.

He whispered a prayer, his heart in his throat.

"That's it!" Adam called. "There's the tree!" His voice carried away on the wind.

They pulled up to the tree, and Cade dismounted before Sutter reached a full stop, steadying Adam as he did.

"It's over there." Adam pointed.

Cade ran for the child-sized hole, and Clay was close behind. It was a squeeze getting through and once he did, the dimness of the cave prevented him from seeing much but the rubble at his feet.

"Get a lantern," he said to Clay. His eyes adjusted to the

darkness, and he carefully made his way through the rubble. "Emily?"

Then he saw her—lying facedown several feet away. Her hair was gray with dirt and gravel, and she lay as still as a corpse.

"Emily!" He rushed to her side, a knot the size of cannon-ball forming in his throat. Why wasn't she moving? Why wasn't she answering? Dread welled up quick and heavy, and his heart sank like a stone.

twenty

A sudden light burst in front of Emily, and she wondered if she were in heaven. A sharp stab of pain relieved her of that notion. She moaned.

"Emily."

She felt someone's hands caressing her face, and she opened her eyes. Blinking against the bright light, she saw a person kneeling beside her. Then she recognized him. "Cade," she whispered. Her parched throat protested.

"It's going to be all right." He asked Clay to go after the doc. "Take Adam with you, will you?"

At his words, she felt relief that Adam had found his pa. She shivered, her body starting odd little tremors that made her leg move and pained her something awful.

"Adam," she whispered.

"He's fine." His voice sounded odd. "I'm going to try to move the rock."

She nodded her head, and the bits of gravel dug into her face with the movement. She sensed him moving toward her feet and braced herself.

"This is going to hurt."

Already the pain had taken her under at least twice. She wondered how much time had passed since—

The weight came off her leg, and searing pain ripped through her. She choked back the scream that came up in her throat. *Please, Lord Jesus, please help me!*

158

A wave of blackness flooded through her, and she fought it with all her will. Her other leg moved restlessly as if it could carry her away from the throbbing limb.

She heard Cade saying something through the fog of pain, and she struggled to focus.

"Doc'll be here soon," he was saying.

Suddenly she wanted to release the tears she'd held for however long she'd lain in this dark chamber. She wanted Cade to take her in his arms and tell her everything was all right.

"It's broken, for sure," he said. "Try to lie still."

As if she could do anything else. She tried to say it, but her tongue felt like it was pasted to the roof of her mouth. "Thirsty."

Cade got up and left, and she felt a sea of hysteria closing over her at the thought of being alone again. Her breath came in shallow puffs. The pain actually seemed worse now that the weight was off. Moments later, he returned and held a canteen to her lips. She drank eagerly of the cool water, though half of it dribbled down her chin and cheek and dripped onto the dirt.

"Be right back." He left her again, and she felt stung once again at his detached tone. Of course he was upset. Worse than upset, and he had a right to be. Hadn't she taken his son where he'd told her not to? Risked his very life with her disobedience?

He must be furious with her. She deserved a broken leg. Why if the boulder had fallen on Adam—she didn't want to think about it. But Cade must have. He blamed her for this, and well he should. How would he ever trust her with Adam again?

It seemed like an eternity before he returned with a blanket and spread it over her wordlessly. She wished he would say something. Hot tears leaked from her eyes and seeped into the soil under her cheek. She'd been so foolish to bring Adam here. Why hadn't she seen it then?

"I'm sorry," she whispered. "I'm so sorry."

"Hush, now."

A clatter outside drew Cade's attention, and she felt alone and cold when he left her again, despite the heavy blanket.

The tremors started again, shooting pain up her leg in fiery darts. She blinked against the pain and tried to call out to Cade, but her lips moved vainly.

The last thing she heard was Doc Hathaway's voice.

❧

Someone was crying and moaning quietly. A low, rumbly voice talked in soothing tones.

A stab of pain brought her fully alert, and she smothered the scream in her throat. Bright lantern light flickered on the armoire at her feet. She was at home in her room.

Doc Hathaway. Cade.

"That oughta do it," the doctor said to Cade.

She looked down at her leg and saw it was splinted. Then she noticed her skirt was pulled clear up to her knee exposing her healthy leg which had ugly blue bruises and several scrapes. Her face grew warm, and she wished she could reach down and cover herself.

"Ah, Mrs. Manning, you're back with us," Doc Hathaway said. An opening in his gray beard exposed his tight smile. To her relief, he pulled the bed's cover up over her legs. "You're going to be just fine. Lucky your husband found you. I've got you all set here and have given you something for the pain."

"Thank you," she whispered.

He smiled and began putting his things in his black bag.

Cade came close, and it was then that she became aware that her face was wet. Tears. She remembered the moaning and crying she'd heard upon awakening and realized it had been her. What had she said in her delirium? Judging from the expression on Cade's face, she'd said something she shouldn't have. No doubt he was still angry.

"I'm so sorry, Cade." Whatever she'd revealed, she owed him an apology. A million apologies. "I know I shouldn't have taken Adam to the cave." How could she even explain why she'd done it without exposing everything about the gold and her uncle?

He nodded. "I already know. About everything—"

"Well," Doc Hathaway said, "I'll be going now. Cade, if I can speak with you a moment."

With one glance back toward her, Cade followed the doctor from the room even as Emily's entire being froze with fear. He knew about the loot. About everything, he'd said. No wonder he was so distant when he found her. He must've gotten the truth from Mara.

Fresh tears welled up in her eyes and clogged her throat. He knew she'd married him only for the gold. He knew she'd used him. She'd found the treasure she'd searched for, but in doing so she had lost what she valued most of all. Her husband's love. He would never have her now. How could he?

And Adam. She would lose the boy she'd come to love as her own son. She put her hands over her face at the realization. An ache, thick and heavy started in her belly at the thought of losing the two people she'd come to love so dearly. Would he turn her away from his home? It was what she deserved.

Others knew where the gold was now, and it would likely be returned to the bank it had been stolen from. How would she save Nana now? *Father, I've made such a mess of things. Why didn't I ask You for guidance? I took it all in my own hands and didn't give You a chance to direct me. And now look what I've done.*

❧

Downstairs, Cade listened to nary a word Doc said about medical instructions. But it hardly mattered since he was scrawling it all on a tablet of paper for Cade.

All he could think about was his wife, lying upstairs in her bed. The most pitiful look had come over her face when he'd told her he knew about everything. He felt awful that he hadn't had time to set her mind at ease before the doctor had called him from the room. Fact was, he hadn't wanted to talk of the loot at all until she was in a better frame of mind. But her mindless ramblings and tears had gotten to him. He could see she was tormented with the secrets she'd held from him. He'd only wanted to set her mind at ease.

When he'd seen her leg in the cave, all purple and blue and bent in a place that had no business bending, he'd wanted to cry himself. But he'd had to be strong for her. He'd seen she was suffering something awful. And as much as he'd wanted to take her in his arms and smother her with kisses, he couldn't deny the guilt he'd felt at having read her diary, at having been privy to her innermost thoughts.

Besides, he'd been afraid to touch her, afraid the slightest movement would pain her even more. He'd been mighty grateful when Doc had given her the morphine.

He looked up the stairs, eager to go check on her, to put her mind at ease about everything. Maybe she was even sleeping soundly now, what with the medicine she had in her.

"Should be about it," Doc was saying as he picked up his bag.

Cade ushered him to the door, thanking the man for his care before heading up the stairs to his wife.

❧

Emily smothered a yawn and forced her eyes to stay open.

Despite all the turmoil going on within her, she felt like she could sleep twelve hours. *Must be the medicine.*

Then she heard sounds outside her door and realized someone was coming up the stairs. Cade, she knew, from the heavy, confident thuds. She wiped her face dry, her heart in her throat. Was he coming to tell her it was over? Would he ask her to leave and never come back?

The door opened, and her husband entered. She absorbed him with her gaze, trying desperately to read him.

He approached the bed. "Doc's gone."

She nodded, her heart pummeling her ribs. The edge of the bed sank as he sat carefully, slowly. A strand of his dark hair hung alongside his stubbled cheek. How could she lose this man, her beloved Cade? Her eyes stung with tears.

"How's your leg feel?"

She was taken back that he still cared enough to ask. "It's not paining much really."

"Good. Doc left more medicine for you when you need it."

The room grew so quiet she could almost hear her fearful heart beating.

"I have some things I need to tell you," he said.

She nodded, unable to speak past the knot that clogged her throat. She must be strong. She mustn't make him feel guilty for his decision. It would only make things harder on him, and she deserved everything she got. She sat as straight as she could against the pillows and steeled herself.

"Last night," he said, "we searched for you for a long time. Adam couldn't find the cave in the dark, and Clay and I. . .well, we did the best we could." He clenched his jaw.

Emily wondered where he was going with this. Her gaze took in his precious face, and she wanted so badly to touch his cheek one last time.

"When we quit for the night, I went back to the Stedmans' and asked Mara some questions. As I said before, I know everything about the loot and your grandmother. About your uncle's plan to get the loot back through you."

He met her gaze just then, and she was shamed by his knowledge. She tucked her chin, and her gaze found the worn quilt. "I'm so sorry," she whispered.

He was quiet so long she wondered if he were going to speak again. Finally, he did. "After that, I came back home. I was angry and I couldn't sleep. I got to thinking maybe the map was in your room someplace, and maybe I could figure out where you were."

She shook her head. "I took it with me."

"I know. I didn't find the map, but I found some other things."

She met his gaze, and his blue-green eyes flickered with something she couldn't identify.

"Your uncle's letters and. . .and your diary."

Her heart did an awkward flop. If he read the letters, he really did know everything. But her diary had private thoughts. Thoughts about him. Her face flooded with heat as she recalled specific things she'd written about her husband.

"I read all the letters—enough to know the sort of man your uncle is." His jaw clenched again, and she wondered if the anger she saw was directed at only her uncle or at her too.

Then he took her hand, and she thought her heart might up and quit right then. What was that shining in his eyes? Dare she hope that—

"I did read a few pages of your diary, and I'm real sorry for poking around in your private things, but. . ." His eyes narrowed with fervency. "You have to understand how confused I was. I was so angry. I felt used. I thought you'd been pretending with me—"

"Pretending?" Her heart caught.

He looked at their joined hands. "I thought you were just using me to get at the loot. That everything was a lie. That your feelings for me were false."

"No. No, that's not true."

He looked at her then. "I know that now. And I can't say as I'm really sorry about reading your diary either. Because if I hadn't, I wouldn't have believed the truth."

Her blood fairly burned with the velvety heat that flowed through her. "I'm not either." And she realized she meant the words. Who cared if he'd read her innermost thoughts if they'd proven her feelings true?

"I was going to tell you something last night, if you recall."

She remembered the embrace they'd shared before she went off to the cave. *Tonight, when Adam's in bed. . .I got some things I want to tell you.* It seemed so long ago, like so many things had gone wrong between then and now. Yet, here her husband was, sitting inches away from her with the same gleam of love in his eyes.

He wet his lips, and she noted how dry her own throat was. "When I married you, as you know, it was to be a marriage of convenience," he said.

His gaze sought confirmation, and she nodded.

"At the beginning, I fought any sort of relationship between us. I guess I was afraid after losing Ingrid and all."

"That's understandable."

His gaze locked on hers, a promise shining in their depths. "Somewhere along the way, I told God I'd put my fear aside.

And after that, my heart didn't stand a chance."

A smile tilted his lips, and she felt it all the way to her heart.

"I love you, Emmie."

She felt her own lips stretch in a smile as joy filled her heart. How could it be, with all the mistakes she'd made, that this man loved her anyhow? She'd lied, used him, risked his son's safety, and still he loved her and wanted her.

Her heart full to overflowing, she blinked back tears. "I love you, Cade. So very, very much."

He leaned toward her then, his lips grazing tenderly over hers, and heat swept through her. Would her pounding heart ever grow accustomed to her husband's touch? She couldn't imagine such a thing. Especially when he touched her cheek so gently.

He broke the kiss, and she almost pulled him back in her arms.

"I want us to be a real husband and wife," he said.

Warmth bathed her face at his meaning.

"I want us to be a real family. The three of us. . .and your grandmother, Lord willing."

Her heart clenched at the thought of Nana. It seemed so hopeless. How could she get Nana back now? The gold would have to be returned to the rightful owners, and rightly so. Her uncle would remain Nana's legal guardian, and after she'd failed to deliver the gold, he would leave Nana in the asylum to spite her.

"Wipe that frown off your face," he said. "I have an idea."

Hope stirred inside her and she searched his eyes. "What is it?"

He shook his head and gave her a tender smile. "Not now, sleepyhead. There'll be time for that later. You need to get some rest—doctor's orders."

"But, I want—"

He held a finger over her lips, and she couldn't resist kissing it. His eyes took on a new look she hadn't seen before. She decided she rather liked it.

"Don't you go doing that, woman."

"Why ever not?" she teased, fighting another yawn.

"Save it for about. . ." He looked pointedly at her splinted leg. "Oh, about six weeks."

She groaned, but he broke it off with a quick kiss. "Doctor's orders."

epilogue

Emily struggled to remove the wedding veil from her elegantly styled up-do. It had been a long, wonderful day. And it wasn't over yet.

"Here, my darling," Cade said from behind her. "Allow me."

She smiled at her husband's reflection in the mirror, taking in the breadth of his shoulders under the crisp, white shirt. His suspenders already dangled from his waistband as if he couldn't wait to shuck the fancy clothes.

"Did I tell you what a beautiful bride you are?"

"Only a dozen times or so." She smiled, content to let him remove her veil. It had been thoughtful of Mara to plan a real wedding for them. Especially for Nana's sake.

As Cade worked the pins out, he bit his lip in concentration. As if reading her thoughts, he asked, "Is Nana settled for the night?"

"Mhmm. She's looking better, don't you think?"

He handed her another pin. "She's filling out, that's for sure."

"She needed to." Just thinking about how Nana had looked when she'd stepped off the stage with Cade was enough to bring tears to her eyes. It had taken months, even with the attorney Cade had hired in Denver, but Nana was home at last.

"It must've been pretty bad at the asylum," he said.

With the veil finally removed, she placed it on the bureau and turned to face him. "Have I told you how thankful I am for what you did?"

"At least a dozen times," he said with a humble smile. "Thanks be to God that the judge saw reason and gave us guardianship of her."

She wrapped her arms around his waist and laid her head on his chest. "Using Uncle Stewart's letters was a brilliant idea."

"I don't know about brilliant, but it worked. His own words were the best proof of his disregard for her."

He tipped her chin up for a peck that lengthened into a satisfying kiss. So much so, that it almost distracted her from the news she'd been waiting to share.

When she pulled away, he caressed her with his gaze. "Something wrong?"

"Not wrong, no."

He tilted his head. "What is it then?"

She soaked in his gaze, eager to see the change that would come over him when he heard the news. "I do have something I need to tell you."

He waited, albeit impatiently if his antsy fingers were anything to go by.

She'd only known for sure for a couple weeks, but somehow, waiting for today seemed right. Suddenly, she giggled.

"What? What is it?"

She put her fingers over her lips. "I never thought I'd say this on my wedding day, much less be thrilled to do so."

"What?" His brows drew low.

"I—I'm in the family way, Cade."

She wished she could forever preserve the expressions that danced across her husband's face. She reveled in each emotion with him.

Finally, he lifted her up off her feet in an airborne embrace and whooped so loudly she feared he'd awaken Adam and Nana.

"Shh!" She swatted him on the shoulder but couldn't hold back the bubble of laughter that welled up in her.

When he was finished whirling around, he let her slide down him until her stockinged feet reached the planked floor. Then his gaze swept over her face in a reflective, serious way.

"I wonder sometimes," he said, "what Thomas would think about all this. You were to be his bride, after all."

She gazed at her husband's precious face, from his clean-shaved jaw to his sea-green eyes, and had trouble imagining herself married to anyone but him. Even her dear friend, Thomas.

"I'm your bride now," she whispered. She let the desire she felt for him blaze from her eyes and was quickly rewarded with that expression she was becoming so wonderfully familiar with.

"Thank you, Ma'am, for that timely reminder," he said, taking her into his arms once more.

A Letter To Our Readers

Dear Reader:

In order that we might better contribute to your reading enjoyment, we would appreciate your taking a few minutes to respond to the following questions. We welcome your comments and read each form and letter we receive. When completed, please return to the following:

Fiction Editor
Heartsong Presents
PO Box 719
Uhrichsville, Ohio 44683

1. Did you enjoy reading *His Brother's Bride* by Denise Hunter?
   ❑ Very much! I would like to see more books by this author!
   ❑ Moderately. I would have enjoyed it more if

   _____

   _____

   _____

2. Are you a member of **Heartsong Presents**?   ❑ Yes   ❑ No
   If no, where did you purchase this book? _____

   _____

3. How would you rate, on a scale from 1 (poor) to 5 (superior), the cover design? _____

4. On a scale from 1 (poor) to 10 (superior), please rate the following elements:

   ____ Heroine   ____ Plot
   ____ Hero   ____ Inspirational theme
   ____ Setting   ____ Secondary characters

5. These characters were special because?_____

_____

_____

6. How has this book inspired your life?_____

_____

_____

7. What settings would you like to see covered in future
   Heartsong Presents books? _____

_____

_____

8. What are some inspirational themes you would like to see
   treated in future books? _____

_____

_____

9. Would you be interested in reading other **Heartsong
   Presents** titles?   ☐ Yes   ☐ No

10. Please check your age range:
     ☐ Under 18   ☐ 18-24
     ☐ 25-34   ☐ 35-45
     ☐ 46-55   ☐ Over 55

Name_____

Occupation _____

Address _____

City_____ State_____ Zip_____

KEY WEST

V isit the historical port of Key West—accessible only by boat—along with an intriguing cast characters from North America and the Caribbean. Share in their search for refuge and hope as they begin new lives on this eight-square-mile island.

Battling forces of nature, human enemies, and their own powerful emotions, four women make their home where Florida meets the sea in wild tropical beauty. Join them on an emotional journey through time to see if faith and love can endure the rough waves of life.

Historical, paperback, 480 pages, 5 3/16" x 8"

❤ • ❤ • ❤ • ❤ • ❤ • ❤ • ❤ • ❤ • ❤ • ❤ • ❤ • ❤

❤ • ❤ • ❤ • ❤ • ❤ • ❤ • ❤ • ❤ • ❤ • ❤ • ❤ • ❤

Presents